T...
my good a...

1

'Second Years!' gloated Barge, banging her bag down on to a desk safely tucked away in a corner of the back row. 'Or Eighth Years,' she added, 'if one chooses to look at it that way.'

'It isn't a question of choosing,' Gerry Stubbs, officious as ever, sanctimoniously corrected her as she squeezed past the Bookends on her way to the front. (Gerry Stubbs liked to sit in the front; she liked to be noticed and answer questions that no one else had a clue to.) 'It's Government orders – it's National Curriculum.'

'Ho! Really?' Barge stood, four square and solid, beside the desk that she had bagged. 'National Curriculum? *Is* it? Well! Fancy! Thank you *so* much for telling me. Where I would have been without that fascinating piece of information I simply cannot imagine. National Curriculum!' she hissed at Bozzy, who was already rootling about under her desk lid.

'You what?' Bozzy emerged, busy and flustered, blue eyes bulging, stubby blond plaits sticking out almost at right angles on either side of her head. 'National Curry Comb?'

People within earshot groaned. Bozzy had taken up

riding last term and had a tendency to relate everything to horses.

'*Curriculum*, dear.' Barge stuck a finger in Bozzy's ear. 'Curree-kew-lum. Got it?'

Bozzy blinked.

'It's obviously beyond her, poor thing.' Barge spoke kindly. 'Don't you worry your little self . . . you just go back under your desk and get on with the mucking out.'

'Well, but I do like to know what is going on,' said Bozzy.

'Patience, my child! All will be revealed, in the fullness of time.'

'All already has been revealed,' said Gerry, 'for those of us who take the trouble to keep abreast.'

'Breast? Did I hear the word *breast*?' That was Melanie, flamboyantly bouncing into the room, followed by her faithful hench people, Ashley and Big Lol. 'Don't tell me somebody has actually *grown* some, at last?'

Julie-Ann Gillon dissolved into giggles. Matty Mc-Shane said, 'That's rude, that is, Melanie Peach. That's personal.'

'Yes,' said Melanie. 'But personal to who?'

'To whom,' said Gerry.

'Heavens!' Melanie gave a theatrical screech. 'Now she's on about wombs! What is this? A Biology lesson?'

'Sex for beginners,' suggested a Bookend. (Emma Gilmore, the larger of the two.)

Fij, sitting next to Jo in the back row, across the gangway from Barge and Bozzy – together the four of them made up the notorious Laing Gang – whispered, 'This sounds as if it's going to be a good term!'

Jo grinned, and nodded. Coming into school with Fij that morning she had seen all the First Years (or Seventh Years, as the case may be) milling about in the courtyard, bleating and twittering, their little universes turned upside down with the shock of being plunged into the hurly-burly of secondary school after the small safe world of Juniors – for Juniors in comparison *had* been small and safe. She had looked back to a year ago and seen herself amongst them, shivering apprehensively with Matty, the lowest of the low, new and nervous and feeling themselves to be so utterly unimportant as to make it almost an impertinence that they were there at all.

Now they were no longer the lowest. They were no longer new, no longer nervous. And even if they could hardly be said, as yet, to rank very high in the scale of importance, at least they were not *quite* nobodies. Last term Jo had even been made form captain, though admittedly it had only been a protest vote on account of people being sick of Gerry Stubbs always bossing them about. Still, it had been an honour in its way. As Barge had rather grandly informed her, 'People who are new to the establishment do not generally get to be *any*thing until they have been here long enough to count as One of Us.'

Having come up from the Homestead, which was the school's junior department, along with Bozzy and Fij and one or two others, Barge had quite naturally regarded the outside contingent as very inferior beings.

Well, she couldn't any more, thought Jo, settling her belongings with some satisfaction in the desk she had bagged for herself and Fij. Second Year, Eighth Year, call it what you will, she had now been here for three whole terms and not even Barge could regard her as an interloper.

The Bookends, sharing a desk to Jo's right, were animatedly discussing who they were likely to have as form mistress.

'I hope it's not Mrs Denver. She's absolute *yuck*.'

'I'd rather have Mrs Denver than Stanny. Stanny's gruesome. She gave Jan Hammond six order marks last term just for looking at her.'

'Just for *looking* at her?'

'She said it was dumb insolence.'

'Just *looking*?'

'That's what she said. She gave her six order marks.'

'But how can –'

The question hung in the air; the door had opened and Mrs Stanley had come in. She directed one of her piercing glances at Emma. Emma promptly shrivelled. The Mouse clapped a hand over her mouth. Jo was so embarrassed for them she felt her own cheeks turn slowly scarlet.

In somewhat grim tones Mrs Stanley said, 'Good morning, 8N.'

Hastily, making amends, they chorused back at her: 'Good morning, Mrs Stanley.'

'Are we all present?'

Even as she spoke, the door opened again the merest crack and a small black shadow slipped through and

4

scurried spiderlike across the room to the nearest vacant desk. A muted giggle rippled through the ranks: Nadge.

'Start as we mean to go on, Nadia,' said Mrs Stanley. 'That is what I always say. What excuse have you fabricated for us this time, so early in the term? Did the bus break down? The traffic lights fail? Or have you managed to concoct something a bit more exotic?'

Nadge was really quite uncrushable. She beamed, happily.

'I was just about to leave when the dog sicked up all over my skirt.'

'Oh! Splendid! That's a new one! How marvellously convenient it must be –' Mrs Stanley said it in tones of sarcastic rapture – 'to have a pet! What will he get up to next, I ask myself? Develop a taste for your Maths homework, maybe? I am warning you here and now,' said Mrs Stanley, reverting to her normal forthright manner of speaking, 'that my tolerance is limited, my fuse is short. Heretofore we have met only for the purposes of rendering you numerate –' Bozzy's eyes popped, uncertainly. 'Or as numerate as some of you are capable of being. Now that we are to be thrown together in circumstances somewhat more intimate for the whole of the coming year – yes, Emma! Your worst fears are fulfilled – I think it may be as well if I state my terms right at the outset. I expect hard work, punctuality, and firmness of purpose. If I get it, all will be well. If I don't – then beware! You have all heard the tale of how I dish out order marks.'

Emma and the Mouse slowly disappeared: Emma

into the neck of her sweater, the Mouse on to the floor to grapple with a shoe lace.

'Good! Now that that is out of the way, we can get down to business.' Mrs Stanley pulled the register towards her. 'Naomi Adams . . . '

Jo sat back, contentedly, in her desk. Mrs Stanley had a reputation for being a terror, but she and Jo, last term, had come to an understanding. Mrs Stanley had finally accepted that Jo genuinely couldn't help being the sort of person who sometimes added up two and two and made it come to five, while Jo in her turn had accepted that it must be very disheartening for Mrs Stanley having to deal with a mathematical moron. They had agreed that Jo didn't set out on purpose to be obtuse, any more than Mrs Stanley set out to cause dismay and perturbation. It was just the way things were.

'So long as we know where we stand,' Mrs Stanley had said, returning Jo's latest Maths homework with 'Rubbish!' written at the bottom of it in rather nasty red ink.

Jo felt, with Mrs Stanley, that she did. She gazed around happily at the rest of 8N. (The *N* stood for Nelligan, which was one of the four Houses at Petersham & St Mary's. The others, all named after former Head Mistresses, were York, Roper and Sutton. Needless to say, Nellie's was vastly superior.)

Fij caught Jo's eye and pulled a face. It didn't specially mean anything, it was just a symbol of togetherness: Jo and Fij against the rest of the world. Jo pulled a face back. She felt comfortable and at home in the cosiness of 8N. There in the back row – counting from the windows across to the door – were Barge, all big and bossy and full of bluster; little pop-eyed Bozzy; medium-sized Jo next to long tall Fij; then the Book-ends, tiny weeny Mouse and pink-bespectacled Emma, inseparable since the Homestead.

In front of Barge and Bozzy were Matty, who had been Jo's best friend at Juniors and still lived next door to her, and Matty's current best friend, Julie-Ann Gillon, more generally referred to as Jool. Next to Matty and Jool were Melanie, who was pretty and very well aware of it and had an uncle who was in a TV soap, and Ashley Wilkerson, who was dim and ordinary and lived in her shade. Next to Ashley was Claire Kramer, who was going to be a ballet dancer, and next to Claire was Nadge, who might have been described as 'the most popular girl in the year' if one were into describing people that way. Nadge was everyone's favourite.

In the front row were the goodies, plus Laurel Busta-mente, who sat simmering and seething in front of Nadge. The reason she was simmering was that she had been separated from Melanie and Ash, and that Ash was sitting next to Melanie, while she was sitting next to Naomi Adams, who was not only a goody but also an intellectual. Her fellow goodies (and intellectuals) were Gerry Stubbs and Pru Frank, sitting just across the gangway. Poor old Lol was going to be left out in the cold. No one could ever have said that Lol was an intellectual. In fact, if there were a bottom band of three, then Lol had to be one of them (the other two being Jool and Bozzy). All the rest jostled along

7

somewhere in between, though last term Jo had actually come top of English, which had shaken Gerry rigid.

After registration they voted as usual for form prefects, which was a bit of a meaningless ritual since the results were always the same: Gerry was always form captain, Nadge was always games. Last term had been a bit of a fluke; no one, least of all Jo, expected that Gerry would be usurped two terms running, and indeed she wasn't. Pru, as usual, nominated her; Gerry, as usual, nominated Pru. The Mouse, being mischievous, said, 'Why don't we have Jammy again?' whereupon Jo, alarmed, gave a squawk of anguish and fell sideways against Fij before picking herself up and retaliating with, 'I nominate Barge – I mean, Margery!'

A wave of exaggerated horror swept the class. Jool and Matty clutched each other, the Bookends garrotted themselves with imaginary ropes. Barge, if anything, was even more hectoring than Gerry. Gerry might be unbearably pious and always *always* in the right; Barge, given her head, could be a down-right bully.

'All right, all right!' Mrs Stanley banged imperiously on her desk lid. She didn't have much patience with the democratic system. Jo felt that she would have far preferred to launch straight into quadratic equations and isosceles triangles than mess around with all this silly business of voting for people. 'That's quite enough time-wasting! Joanne, do you want to stand for form captain or not?'

'Um –' Jo struggled for a moment. On the one hand it had undeniably given one a tremendous feeling of

8

importance, having a badge with *Form Captain* pinned to one's chest and going along to House meetings and being treated as a somebody. On the other hand the strain of being perpetually on one's best behaviour and striving to set good examples *at all times*, when one was not by nature a good-example-setting sort of person, had really been incredibly wearing.

'Well?' said Mrs Stanley.

'Um – no, it's all right,' said Jo, 'thank you. I think this term I'll stay as I am.'

'I'll stand,' said Barge.

There was a giggle from Fij, groans from the Book-ends.

Mrs Stanley turned, somewhat wearily, to the black-board. '*Margery Laing*,' she wrote. Jool and Matty fell forward on their desk lids in mock faints. 'Right! Any more suggestions? Good, then let's get on and vote.'

They voted. Surprise, surprise! Gerry was form cap-tain, Pru was vice.

'The heavy mob,' moaned Barge, as they emerged into the playground at break. (Jo thought this quite funny: Barge would have been a heavy mob practically on her own.) 'This is going to be a *disaster*. If only you hadn't gone and got cold feet –' she rounded accusingly on Jo – 'we'd have been all right. I could have been captain, you could have been my second-in-command.'

There was a pause.

'I don't see how you work that out,' said Fij, 'con-sidering there was only one person that voted for you.'

'Obviously –' Barge said it loftily – 'if Jammy had

stood alongside me the voting pattern would have been quite different.'

'Yes,' said Bozzy, 'we'd all have voted for Jam.'

Bozzy said these things quite innocently – at least, Jo supposed that she did. It was hard to be sure, with Bozzy. You sometimes asked yourself, could anyone really be that naive?

'We'd have had Jammy for form captain –' Bozzy smiled seraphically at Jo, totally missing the murderous glare that Barge was giving her – 'and we'd have had a really *nice* term, like last term was.'

'It wasn't all that nice,' said Jo. 'Not at the beginning. . . . You all hated me.'

'Yes, but we got used to you,' said Bozzy.

'Well, I didn't get used to me. I don't want to have to keep putting people down and being good all the time. I want to have fun!'

'Does that mean you're going to break out and go mad?' said Bozzy, hopefully.

'No. I'm going to *achieve* things.'

'What sort of things?'

'Oh! I don't know! Whatever there is to achieve.' The Under-14 netball team, for a start; definitely House, maybe even school. That was one thing she was determined on – especially as she had been voted vice games. (She had won by a narrow margin over Fij. She hoped Fij didn't mind too much, though even if she did she wasn't the sort of person to bear a grudge. Not like Barge, who could be implacable.) 'Let's go and see who the House captains are!'

Against all the rules – only nobody minded too much

on the first day of term – they went stampeding back into school, down the main corridor to the House notice boards. There they clattered to a halt in horror and revulsion.

'Michelle Wandres?'

'Michelle *Wandres*?'

'Michelle WANDRES?'

'Oh, but this is grotesque!' cried Barge.

'What is she *doing* here? Why hasn't she *gone*?'

Bozzy was running in circles, pitiably flapping her hands. Jo knew how she felt. She might almost have started running in circles herself, if it weren't for the fact that it looked rather silly and you never knew who might be watching. But Michelle Wandres as House captain – horrible!

'I'll tell you why she hasn't gone.' Barge hissed it, venomously. 'It's because she's *stupid* . . . she obviously failed *all* her A levels and has had to come back and retake them!'

'On the contrary, you obnoxious little worm!'

The voice spoke from behind them. Jo and Fij spun round in confusion. Bozzy stopped, half way round one of her circles, eyes bulging, mouth agape, hands held up like bunny paws beneath her chin. Barge made a kind of whumpfing noise down her nose.

'Mitch –' *Mitch*! – 'is one of the brightest people in the whole House. She didn't fail her A's because she's stupid but because her brother very tragically died. I don't know whether your juvenile imaginations can cope with that concept . . . you sound as if you're too immature and ignorant to understand what it can do

11

to a person. But in future, just don't be so quick to jump to conclusions! Now, if you wouldn't mind getting out of my way . . . '

Jo, in her haste to comply, tripped over one of her own feet and went sprawling; Fij promptly fell on top of her. Barge whumpfed again, somewhat defiantly, but none the less shifted her bulk. Bozzy slowly closed her mouth and brought her hands down to her sides.

'Thank you!'

The newcomer – Jo didn't remember seeing her before in all the time she had been at Peter's – leaned forward to pin a notice on the board. She was evidently a prefect, for she was wearing the red-and-silver tie that only prefects wore. She looked exactly, but *exactly*, the way that Jo would have given anything to look: slim, medium height – which was by far the best, really, because who wanted to be a midget like Mouse or a walking beanpole like Naomi? – with curly dark hair cut very short, the sort of face which you could swear had been made to measure, with sculpted cheekbones and everything perfectly in proportion (no lopsided nose or baggy mouth or any of the niggling imperfections that ordinary people had to carry round with them) deep-brown eyes with thick sooty lashes and a dusky-pink complexion which might have come out of a bottle except that somehow you could tell that it hadn't.

Jo stared, and couldn't stop. How blissful life would be if one looked like that! Never having to pinch at one's nose to try and make it a better shape, never having to stretch at one's mouth in a vain attempt to promote width, never having to look in the mirror and see *freckles*.

'Well!' Barge whumpfed again, indignantly this time, as the glorious personage whisked herself away down the corridor. 'It seems one can never conduct a private conversation in this place without some busybody *ear-holing*.'

'Who is she?' said Jo. Her voice sounded faint and far away. Fij looked at her, curiously.

Barge said, 'Search me.'

Bozzy, having completed her half-finished circle and ended up at the notice board, peered short-sightedly at the notice which the Glorious P. had just pinned there. She said, 'Sarah Bigg.'

'Sarah Bigg?' Jo felt a momentary twinge of disappointment. Bigg was hardly the surname one would have chosen for a glorious personage. Of course, Bozzy was notoriously unreliable – they had spent the whole of last term addressing one of the prefects as Proline, all because of Bozzy – but it was hard to see how even she could make a mistake over a simple name like Bigg.

'And who,' demanded Barge – *sniff*! – 'is Sarah Bigg when she's at home?'

Bozzy peered again. 'House games captain.'

'House *games* captain? How can a perfect stranger come waltzing in from nowhere and be made House games captain?'

'I don't know,' said Bozzy, 'but that's what it says.'

'Oh, get out of the way!' Barge pushed at her, impatiently. 'Let me have a look.'

Barge looked.

'So what does it say?' said Fij.

'*Sarah Bigg – House Games Captain.*'

'I told you,' said Bozzy.

'Oh, shut up!' said Barge.

'Sarah Bigg,' said Fij, in tones of wonderment.

Definitely, *definitely*, thought Jo, she was going to make that Under-14 netball team . . .

2

'Do you suppose,' said Jo, at the tea table that evening, 'that I could have a netball?'

Her words were lost in the sudden angry bellow of her brother Tom across the table: 'This pizza's got a slug in it!'

'Where?' Mrs Jameson leaned over, indignantly, to look.

'There!' Tom stabbed with his fork. 'That black thing!'

'Eat it,' advised Andy. 'Do you good. Nice bit of protein . . .'

'*Do* you?' said Jo.

'Do I what?' said her mother, preoccupied.

'Think I could have a netball!'

'Ask me at Christmas. Tom Jameson, that is not a slug, it's a piece of olive!'

'Olive?' Tom prodded at it, suspiciously. 'Looks like a slug to me.'

'Well, it's not! Get on and eat it.'

Tom pulled a face. 'Don't like olives. They taste of snot.'

'So do slugs,' said Andy. 'I expect.'

'I think it *is* a slug . . . look, it's moving!'

'I really need a netball,' said Jo.

'Christmas,' said her mother. It was what she automatically said to any request that involved money – *ask me at Christmas, at Easter, on your birthday.*

'I need it *now*,' said Jo.

'You always need everything now. You needed ballet shoes now, and ice skates now, and a mouth organ now. . . . If I bought you everything you suddenly took a fancy to, we'd all end up on the streets. Tom, stop that!'

Tom had just flicked his slug across the table at Andy, who caught it neatly and popped it in his mouth.

'Yum-yum, nice gollop of snot!'

Honestly, thought Jo; boys were so childish. You'd never believe, from the way they carried on, that Tom was a year her senior and that Andy was sixteen.

'Christmas will be too late,' she said. 'We only play netball for this term. After that it's hockey.'

'Then, I suppose, you'll be screaming for a hockey stick!'

'*Could* I?' said Jo.

'Christmas.'

Jo sighed. One had to be patient. 'Suppose I had the hockey stick for Christmas and the netball for my birthday? Except that if you gave it to me now it would probably be cheaper than giving it to me on my *actual* birthday because that would mean waiting till February, and you know what Dad's always saying about inflation.'

'She's right,' said Andy, coming to her aid as he sometimes did. 'Cost you the price of a Rolls-Royce if you wait till February.'

'It is *very* important,' said Jo.

'It's always very important. The ballet shoes were important. The ice sk–'

'This is *really* important.' The ice skates had been a mere passing phase, and the ballet shoes had been when she was under the influence of Claire. Netball was something that lasted. 'Really, *really*,' said Jo.

'Why? What's so really really about it?'

'Well, because if I don't have a netball I won't be able to practise, and if I don't practise I won't get into the team.'

'And what about all those girls whose parents can't afford to buy them netballs? What happens to them?'

'They don't get into the team!' said Tom. He cackled and speared a piece of pizza on the edge of his fork.

Jo bit her lip. 'Some of them get into the team.' Nadge didn't have a netball and she got into all sorts of teams. But then Nadge was special. Jo was just a bit better than most people – so long as she practised. She *had* to practise! She couldn't bear it if from now until the end of time Sarah Bigg simply thought of her as one of the girls who was mean about Michelle Wandres.

'Oh, Mum, *please*!' she said.

'I'll make a bargain with you. . . . If you and Tom can manage to go for the rest of the week without having a fight, you can have your netball.'

Jo looked at her, dubiously. Was it possible to go a whole week without fighting him? Tom was so horridly rebarbative. (A nice new word that she had learnt

17

during the summer holidays. It meant ghastly and repellent.)

'Of course,' said Mrs Jameson, 'it would mean that both of you would have to make a conscious effort to be a bit more civilized.'

'What's in it for me?' said Tom. 'If she's having a netball, what am I having?'

'Nothing! You've just had a new pair of football boots.'

There was a silence; then: 'A-hem!' said Andy, elaborately clearing his throat.

'Tom did need football boots,' pleaded Mrs Jameson.

'I need my netball!' said Jo.

'Jo needs her netball,' said Andy.

'That's right, take her side!' roared Tom.

Jo flicked her eyes anxiously from Andy to her mother.

'Dad and I,' said Andy, 'are going in to get some new golf balls Saturday morning.'

'Really?' Mrs Jameson said it weakly. Jo knew, then, that the battle was as good as won.

'She could always come in with us, if she wanted.'

'Mum?' Jo spun round, breathlessly, on her chair.

'Oh, all right!' Mrs Jameson caved in, just as she always did when there was any hint of unfairness.

'Hurray!' yelled Tom. 'That means we can fight all we want!'

'It means nothing of the sort,' said Mrs Jameson. 'And you, my girl, had just better get into that team!'

'I'm going to get a netball,' Jo told Matty, as they went into school together the next morning.

'What for?' said Matty.

'So that I can practise! We can *both* practise. Dad said if I like he'll fix up a net in the garden. You could come in and practise shooting.'

'Mm.' Matty sounded distinctly lukewarm at the prospect. Ever since she had become best friends with Jool and taken up photography she seemed to have lost interest in playing netball or hockey and getting into teams.

'If we practised really hard,' said Jo, seeking to encourage, 'we might make the school Under-14s.'

'Don't think I'd want to,' said Matty. 'Haven't really got the time. It was bad enough last year, being in the House team . . . all those extra practices Elizabeth kept making us go to.'

'That was Elizabeth,' said Jo. 'It's Sarah Bigg now.'

'Who's Sarah Bigg?' Matty asked.

'Games captain,' said Jo.

'Oh?' Matty looked at her. (Jo tried hard not to blush.) 'I've never heard of her.'

'She's been in America for a year, with her parents.'

It was Lol who had supplied the information. The Lollipop's dad ran a restaurant, and Sarah Bigg's parents, according to Lol, were two of his best customers. Lol quite often came up with odd snippets about people. She listened in on her mum and dad's private conversations and then relayed them to anyone who cared to listen. Generally Jo tried to remain aloof from the Lollipop's gossip, but she hadn't been able to stop her ears flapping at the mention of Sarah.

'She's a really brilliant person,' Lol had reported at the dinner table yesterday to Melanie and Ash. 'She did absolutely brilliantly in America. They all wanted her to stay over there, she was so brilliant.'

'So why didn't she?' Melanie had asked.

'Out of loyalty to Peter's.' Lol had announced it with an air almost proprietorial: as if she herself were in some way linked to Sarah and her brilliance. 'She's a really really nice person, as well as being absolutely fantastic at games and having this fantastically brilliant brain.'

Jo felt that all this was very possibly true. Sarah must be good at games, or she wouldn't have been made captain; and she must be a nice person, or she wouldn't have leapt to the defence of Mealy Mouth Wandres. She most probably did have a fantastic brain, or at any rate Jo was quite willing to believe that she did. Nevertheless, she had a certain sympathy with Melanie's retort, 'So what do they call her? Superwoman?' There was no denying Lol's tendency to gush.

Jo wasn't going to gush. Carefully she said: 'She was in the senior netball team when she was still only in the Fourth Form.'

'You mean Year 11,' corrected Matty.

'No, I don't. I mean the *Fourth* form! National Curriculum hadn't been invented then.' It was really very irritating when people nitpicked. What did it matter what you called it? Fourth Form, Year 11, it was still a remarkable feat, making the senior netball team at the age of only fourteen. Or maybe fifteen. She wondered when Sarah's birthday was. Lol would probably know, or could find out, but she hadn't yet sunk so low as to go round asking questions of Lol.

'Nadge says she can remember seeing her play when she was in the Homestead – when Nadge was in the Homestead, I mean. She said she was brill.' And if Nadge said she was brill, you could believe it; Nadge didn't gush like Lol.

'Yeah?' Matty shifted her school bag from right hand to left. 'Know what?' she said. 'I'm thinking of going in for a photography competition. What it is, you've got to take pictures of people and their animals – except I don't know any people with animals. Do you know any people with animals?'

Jo tutted, impatiently. She was obviously wasting her time: Matty wasn't in the least bit interested either in netball or in Sarah.

'Pet animals,' said Matty. 'D'you know anyone with a pet animal?'

'Yes!' Jo went zipping off up Shapcott Road in pursuit of Fij. 'Why don't you go and take a picture of Bozzy and her horse?'

'That's an idea!' said Matty.

On Saturday morning Jo went into town with Andy and her dad to buy her netball. They went into Wilmer's – *WILMER'S of London, Paris & Petersham* – which had a good sports department where Andy and Mr Jameson could also buy their boring golf balls. (Golf

21

was such a dreary game; no running or passing or tackling. Jo couldn't see the point of it.)

On their way out of the store, as they turned into the arcade which would take them to the central shopping precinct, with Jo proudly carrying her new netball in its net, a hand suddenly descended on Jo's shoulder and a voice cried, 'Jolly good!'

Jo spun round.

'Going to put in some extra practice?' said Sarah. She smiled at Jo. (Had she already forgiven her for being one of the girls who was mean about Michelle?)

Jo dimpled and tried not to blush.

'That's the stuff!' said Sarah. She was wearing a polo-neck sweater and an anorak, with riding breeches and long boots. It suited her even better than school uniform. 'Thinking of trying for one of the teams?'

Jo nodded, shyly.

'Great!' Sarah stuck up a thumb. 'See you at the trials.'

Sarah moved off, with easy athletic stride, through the Saturday morning crowds, leaving Jo all of a happy fluster, beaming and twinkling and radiating pinkness. Andy, too, was rather pink, though Jo didn't really notice it at the time.

'So who was that sporty young goddess?' said Mr Jameson.

'She's our House games captain,' said Jo.

'Who is she?' said Andy. 'What's her name?'

'Sarah Bigg.' Jo said it blissfully. The more used to it she became, the more right it sounded.

'Sarah *Bigg*?' said Mr Jameson.

22

Jo looked at him, rather haughtily. 'That is what she is called.'

'Good grief!' Her dad laughed. Jo wanted to hit him.

'What's in a name?' said Andy.

'You tell me!' said Mr Jameson.

'"A rose by any other name . . . "'

Mr Jameson choked. 'Oh dear, oh lor!' he said. 'This is more than I can take!'

Jo and Andy looked at each other.

'She's really nice,' said Jo, earnestly. 'You could come and watch her play sometime if you'd like to.'

'I might just do that,' said Andy.

On Monday Gerry went to a House meeting and came bustling self-importantly back to announce that 'Michelle expects, now we are Eighth Years, that our behaviour will be a bit more adult than it has been in the past . . . she says that last year it was a disgrace and that this year she is not going to put up with it.'

The class listened in glum (in some cases) or rebellious (in other cases) silence. Last year's head of House had been Kay Wyman, studious and rather aloof, not terribly concerned with the rumbustious antics of the first years. Kay had tolerated behaviour which they knew, even without Gerry's sanctimonious warning, Michelle never would. Michelle had always been mean. The sort of person, thought Jo, who got a positive enjoyment from picking on people. Of course it was horrible for her, if her brother had died: Jo couldn't bear the thought of anything happening to Tom or Andy. Tom might be totally and utterly repulsive, and

23

there might be times when she loathed him, but she still wouldn't want him getting a brain tumour or being run over or anything like that. On the other hand, according to Katy Wells in Year 9, Michelle had been mean ever since anyone could remember. She would be even worse now she was in a position of power.

'*Any*way –' Gerry raised her voice as a mutinous murmuring broke out in the corner of the room where Barge, Bozzy and the Bookends were gathered – 'Michelle said I was to give you due warning. We want to win the Dorothy Beech this year . . . right?'

Pru said 'Right!' and one or two people gave half-hearted cheers. The cheers were half-hearted because winning the Dorothy Beech Cup, whilst pleasing enough in theory, would in practice entail being on their best behaviour from now until the end of the school year; a feat which held no attractions whatso-ever either in theory or in practice, and would, more-over, almost certainly be beyond them. 8N's capacity for good behaviour was strictly limited.

'One way we can help,' bawled Gerry, quelling the would-be mutineers by sheer force of personality (Gerry, unlike Jo, was a natural dictator), 'is by volun-teering t– '

'Never volunteer!' shouted a heckler from the corner. The voice shouted like Emma's.

' – *volunteering*,' said Gerry, 'to go on tidiness patrol in the cloakrooms and by keeping our own classroom free of clutter. The way some people,' she said, looking rather pointedly in Bozzy's direction, 'make a pigsty of their surroundings is beyond a joke.' (Indignant

24

spluttering and snorting from the corner, ignored by Gerry.) 'Another way of helping is by taking part in as many House activities as we can. Games, of course, is up to Nadge, so I won't say anything about that –'

'Hurray!' squeaked the Mouse. Someone blew a raspberry, someone else stamped her feet. Gerry drew herself up.

'I won't say anything about *that*, but what I will say is that some people round here have a quite extraordinary way of conducting themselves, grunting and squawking and going off like popguns. *If*,' said Gerry, 'there is something wrong with your internal organs –' smothered giggle from the corner – 'might I suggest you go along to the Office and ask to be looked at straight away before you blow up or something? We don't want a mess all over the walls. We are *trying*,' she reminded them, 'to win the Dorothy Beech.'

'And anyway,' said Lol, 'I'm tidiness monitor. I'm not going to clear up someone's horrible innards.'

'You'd have to, if they blew up,' pointed out Barge.

'I jolly well would not! They could clear it up themselves.'

'Don't see how they could, if they'd blown up.'

'Th– '

'*Look here*!' Gerry thundered with her fist on a desk lid. 'Just shut up and listen, will you, when a person's trying to speak!'

'Heavens!' said Bozzy. 'I thought she'd finished.'

'I have one final important announcement to make. The prefects,' said Gerry, 'have got together and written something for the end-of-term show. They're going to put it in for the interhouse drama award, which as you know carries a simply whacking great number of points and would help enormously in our battle for the Cup. I therefore consider it the duty,' wound up Gerry, 'of anyone with even the glimmerings of dramatic talent to put their names down for auditions and get themselves a part if they possibly can. Jasmine Patel is going to direct, and she has already told me that she is specially looking to us for support, knowing as she does,' said Gerry, 'that we have a Potential Star in our midst.'

Melanie smiled, modestly, and tilted her head to get it at its most flattering angle. The Lollipop and Ashley applauded. Barge, as they swarmed out towards the playground, gave a derisive honk.

'They needn't think they're getting me auditioning for them! After last time?' She trumpeted, witheringly, down her nose. 'I'd sooner go and sit on a chimneypot and gibber! I wouldn't take part in another of their childish productions if they went on their bending knees and *begged* me.'

'Which on the whole they are not very likely to do,' said Fij, consolingly, 'so I don't expect you'll actually have to go and sit on any chimneypots.'

'I didn't say I would *have* to. I said I would *rather*.' Barge spoke testily. Why couldn't people *listen*? 'All I'm saying is that if they want someone to go and make a laughing stock of themself they can jolly well look elsewhere.'

'Yes, they jolly well can!' said Bozzy. She nodded

her plaits vehemently. 'They had their goose and cooked it.'

'Precisely,' said Barge. 'All this stuff about *duty* . . . they needn't think that washes any curtains with *me*. And that,' she added, 'goes for all of us, I should hope.'

The manner in which Barge expressed hope was definitely threatening rather than pious. Fij hastened to assure her: 'It certainly goes for me.'

'Jammy?'

Barge fixed her gaze, basilisk-like, upon Jo.

'Um – well,' said Jo.

It was true that last time they had all felt themselves somewhat ill-used, having been cast, to their initial satisfaction, as fairies in *A Midsummer Night's Dream*, only to discover at the eleventh hour, when it was too late to do anything about it, that they had been put in solely as light relief and were being made to look decidedly stupid (trailing hems and broken wands and *Wellington boots*), but even so it had turned out to be quite fun, once one had accepted that one was there to be laughed at rather than admired. And Jo did still have rather a hankering to get up on stage.

'They are different people,' she pleaded. 'Jasmine Patel is not Wendy Armstrong.'

'That is hardly a revelation,' said Barge. 'I dare say even Bozzy may have noticed *that*.'

'Yes, I had.' Bozzy spoke eagerly, happy for once to be up with the action. 'And I'll tell you something else that Jasmine Patel isn't, she isn't Jasmine Patel. Her name isn't Jasmine at all, it's Jas – Jas something

27

else,' said Bozzy, petering out. 'I saw it written down. I can't remember what it was, but it's not Jasmine.'

'What's that got to do with it?' said Barge. 'She could be called Daffodil or Lilac for all I care.'

'It's not Daffodil or Lilac. It's like Jasmine only not. Jaswija, or –'

'Glaswegian?' said Fij, trying to be helpful.

'Look, will you just belt up!' cried Barge. 'It doesn't matter what she's called, it's the principle of the thing.' Principles were very important to Barge, especially when it was the principle of people doing what she wanted them to do. 'It would be nothing less than an act of gross treachery –' she addressed herself sternly to Jo – 'if you were to go and act for them.'

Jo sighed. 'Well, I don't expect I will,' she said, 'because I dare say Melanie will be the only person they'll want – and Claire, if there's any dancing. I don't expect they'll really be interested in any of the rest of us.'

'Even if they were,' said Barge, 'we should expect you to stand firm.'

'Oh, absolutely!' said Jo. It was always easiest to tell Barge what she wanted to hear. It saved a lot of unpleasantness. 'Shall I go and get my netball and we could practise?'

It was while they were running up and down the playground, passing to one another, that Sarah appeared, walking across from the Hut (where Year 13 had most of their classes) together with Jasmine Patel and Michelle Wandres. Michelle as usual was looking disagreeable – it was something, Jo supposed,

28

that she just couldn't help. She had probably been doing it so long that her face had got stuck like it. Sarah and Jasmine were deep in discussion, but all the same Sarah broke off as they skirted past the four netball players.

'That's what I like to see! Keep it up!'

Jo beamed and blushed and radiated like a beacon. The remark had been directed at her, she was almost sure of it.

'Well, I suppose she is at least halfway human,' said Barge, grudgingly. 'Elizabeth was more classy –' more classy? What cheek! – 'but one always felt she regarded one as something rather nasty that had fallen out of a dustbin. I say, Jam, did you know you'd gone the most peculiar colour?'

'Me?' said Jo.

'Yes, you look like a big ripe strawberry.'

'Or a tomato,' said Fij.

'Or a radish,' said Bozzy.

They all three stood and watched as Jo's face turned rapidly from pink to rose to deepest crimson.

'You surely haven't got a *thing*,' said Fij, 'about Sarah Bigg?'

'She has, she has!' crowed Bozzy.

'I haven't,' said Jo.

'Then why have you gone that very odd colour?'

'I get like this sometimes,' said Jo, desperately. 'It's to do with my metabolism.'

'Ho, ho, pull the other one!' Barge snatched the netball and chucked it triumphantly at Fij. '*Sar*ah Bigg, *Sar*ah Bigg, Jam's got a thing about *Sar*ah Bigg!'

Jo screeched and hurled herself on the ball. If Barge didn't stop shouting, the whole school would know.

3

Over the weekend, Jo's dad had fixed up a hoop in the back garden for Jo and Matty to practise their shooting.

'What I *really* need to practise,' said Jo, as they raced back from school on Monday afternoon, 'is passing.' Matty was the shooter, not Jo. It was easier for Matty, being so much taller – at least, that was Jo's theory. The nearer the goal you were, the more chance you had of getting the ball in; it stood to reason. 'Let's start from down at the house, and pass all the way up to the rockery, then you can practise a few shots, and then –'

'Yeah, all right,' said Matty. She tossed the ball. 'Let's get on with it.'

On Monday they practised until it was almost too dark to see. On Tuesday Matty said there was something she wanted to watch on television, on Wednesday she made the excuse that she had too much homework, on Thursday she came in for just ten minutes then said she'd suddenly remembered something important that she'd got to do indoors. Matty had never been as keen on games as Jo; now it seemed she wasn't keen at all.

In the end Jo gave up and practised by herself, which meant practising shooting since there really wasn't anything else you could do on your own. To make it more interesting she divided herself into teams – Fij, Jo and Nadge on one team, Barge, Bozzy and Matty on the other. Then she tried shooting in different styles, according to which person she was being. Then Tom came out and started interfering and boasting about how easy it was and how anyone that wasn't half blind could get a ball that size through a hoop that size and snatched at the ball to prove it and promptly discovered that he couldn't, so then Jo and Tom had a shooting match against each other, which Jo won by twenty-two goals to fifteen, which Tom said didn't mean anything because of her having practised, to which Jo retorted that Tom was taller than she was and anyhow he was a boy, and weren't boys supposed to be superior at absolutely everything?

'Not at girls' games!' yelled Tom. 'Netball's really naff!'

'Then why did you come out here in the first place?' shrieked Jo. 'Why couldn't you just leave me alone?'

''Cause I felt sorry for you, all by yourself!'

'No, you didn't, you just wanted to come and show off, 'cause you thought it was·so easy!'

'It is easy,' said Tom. 'That's why I couldn't be bothered doing it properly. It's a kids' game.'

'Andy doesn't think so,' said Jo. 'Andy's going to come and watch us play sometime.'

'Andy's a nerd,' said Tom.

Jo hurled the netball at him. Tom put up a hand and punched; the netball rose into the air and sailed neatly over the wall into next door's garden. Jo screeched:

'Now look what you've done! You can jolly well go and get it!'

'Get it yourself,' said Tom.

Later that evening, after she had meekly gone next door (not Matty's, but the other side) and been lectured by an angry neighbour on the subject of netballs landing on top of flowerbeds and crushing the flowers, Jo said: 'Are boys of a certain age always rebarbative, do you think?'

Her mum and dad both laughed. Andy said, 'I object to that! I'm not.' Tom didn't say anything because of being too ignorant to know what the word meant. He just sat and stared at the television and to Jo's satisfaction turned a sullen red all the way from the neck up.

'He'll grow out of it,' said Mr Jameson. 'How's the netball? Have you got into that team yet?'

'Not yet,' said Jo. 'The trials aren't till next week.'

'So who says who gets in? Big Sal?'

It was Jo's turn to blush. She shook her hair over her face, but not before Tom had seen. He pounced.

'Look at her! She's gone all like a lobster! Who's Big Sal?'

'Nothing to do with you!' said Jo. And anyway, she wasn't called Sal; she was Sarah. Sal was horrible.

'Is she the games captain? Are you in love with her?'

'Don't be *stupid*,' snarled Jo.

'I bet you are! I bet you're in love with her! Girls are always falling in love with each other.'

'It's a sight better than fighting each other,' said Mrs Jameson.

Tom had always been getting into fights when he

33

was younger. The mothers of other boys had come almost daily to the house to complain that 'your son hit my son in the eye', or 'your son threatened to punch my son's teeth down his throat', or 'your son threw my son's football boots on to the railway line'.

'I'm going to tell Robbie,' said Tom, conveniently ignoring his mother's remark. 'I'm going to tell him you've thrown him over for a *girl*!'

'I'd throw Robbie over for Sarah Bigg,' said Andy.

'Sarah Bigg?' Tom latched on to it, delightedly. 'Is that her name? Sarah Bigg? Sarah Bigg, grunts like a pig – *oink*, *oink*!'

Tom made a series of loud slurping grunting noises. Jo looked crossly at her dad. It was his fault, talking about Big Sal – trying to be funny, just like always. Men were *idiots*.

Next day at school, the Laing Gang were preparing for their usual lunch-time mooch about the playground – Barge having decreed that netball was all very well *in its place*: 'We don't want to get narrow-minded. I should like to think we could enjoy a bit of intelligent conversation from time to time' – when Sarah came sprinting past in T-shirt and shorts.

'Not practising today?' She threw it over her shoulder as she headed for one of the courts. 'You wait till you're under my command!'

Even Barge had to admit that the remark seemed to have been addressed specifically at Jo.

'Well! If that isn't as good as *telling* you you've got a place in the team. I am sure,' said Barge, ruffling slightly, 'we all know how these things work.'

'How?' said Bozzy.

'Oh! People having their favourites . . . that sort of thing.'

Jo couldn't decide whether to savour the idea – could she really be one of Sarah's favourites? But if so, how? She hadn't *done* anything – or whether to treat it as an insult and take umbrage. Fortunately, Fij took umbrage for her.

'It isn't anything to do with having favourites. She knows Jam's got a netball, she knows she's been practising, she knows she was in last year's Under-13s –'

'We were all,' said Barge, 'in last year's Under-13s. And we have all,' she said, 'been practising.'

'Yes, and how does she know whose netball it is, anyway?' added Bozzy, with more than a hint of aggression.

'She saw me with it.' Jo said it apologetically. 'When I'd just bought it.'

'Oh.' said Bozzy. 'Did she? I see. Yes. Well.'

'That does nothing to alter the fact –' Barge spoke on a note of rising irritability – 'that we have all of us been practising. Do I have to repeat myself? We – have – all – of – us –'

' – been practising,' said Fij, soothingly. 'That's right.'

'It most certainly *is* right.'

'Precisely,' said Bozzy. She looked at Jo with big soup-plate eyes. Barge folded her arms.

'I rest my case,' said Barge.

Jo wrestled for a moment with the saintly notion of saying that in her opinion Sarah had obviously intended

35

to include all four of them, decided even in the act of opening her mouth that she wasn't feeling that generous, and changed it to, 'Actually, I'm going to try for the Under-14s this time.'

'Oh! Go right to the top,' said Barge. 'Why not?'

'Well, I *could* still play for the Under-13s, but –'

'You want to be noticed by *Her*.'

'I wasn't thinking of being noticed,' said Jo, gently reproachful. 'I was thinking of the House.'

They regarded her, pityingly.

'Well!' said Bozzy. 'That is just so *pathetic* –'

'You don't have to pretend in front of us,' said Barge, kindly. '*We know*.'

Jo's blushful bleat of 'Know what?' was drowned by a sudden cascade of giggles from Fij.

'I was talking to my gran last night. . . . She said when she was at school she had this terrific thing about a girl called Margaret Spry, all because she had a brace on her teeth.'

'Because she had a *brace* on her teeth?'

'Yes. She said it made her say her *S*s in a funny way, like *thish*. My gran said she thought it was ever so romantic. She even asked her parents if she could have one, and they said no, she didn't need it, so what she used to do, she used to go to bed every night with an elastic band round her front teeth trying to make them grow crooked so the dentist would say she'd got to.'

'Way out!' said Barge.

'Well, she was only eleven,' said Fij. 'By the time she was our age she'd stopped having a thing about tooth braces and started having a thing about boys.'

'She can keep *boys*,' said Barge. 'I'd sooner have a thing about a hole in the road than about a *boy*.'

'Oh, me too!' agreed Fij. 'But anyway in her day they didn't call it a thing, they called it a pash.'

'Pash!' gurgled Bozzy. 'What's a pash?'

'What Jammy's got.'

'I haven't!'

'Short for *passion*, dear.'

'I haven't!'

'*Pash*,' gloated Bozzy. 'Jammy's got a *pash*.'

'I h–'

'Oh, do stop trying to deny it!' said Barge. 'It's so pointless – especially when you go bright beetroot every time you see her!'

As a rule, on a Friday evening Jo went to the Youth Club with Matty and Tom, and sometimes with Jool and Matty's brother Miles. This Friday she was still in the garden practising her shooting when Matty called round.

'She's besotted,' said Tom. 'She wants to get into the team and be with Sarah Bigg.'

'Oh, yeah?' said Matty, unimpressed. Matty was going through a hate-men phase. She and Jool, over the holidays, had decided that boys were trash and they didn't want anything to do with them. 'Maybe she just wants to get into the team 'cause she just wants to get into the team.'

'That's what you think,' said Tom.

'What's it to you, anyway?' said Matty. Deliberately she turned her back on him. 'You coming, Jam?'

'Dunno.' Jo, even now, was in two minds. The Club was fun – but so was practising. And after four evenings on her own with a netball and a goal post she was starting to get really good. She had been in the middle of a private contest – one hundred tries, odd numbers against even – when Matty had arrived. So far, the odd numbers had scored ten, the evens fifteen. She would rather like to have gone on and finished. 'I'm not changed,' she said.

'What's it matter? It's only the Club. There's nobody there –' Matty threw a contemptuous glance in Tom's direction – 'of any importance. Least, not as far as I'm aware.'

There was Robbie, of course. Robbie was in Tom's class at school and he and Jo had been going-out-sort-of for ages and ages, ever since February, when he had come to her birthday party. Everyone accepted that he was her boyfriend; sort of. It had to be sort of because Jo's mother, who sometimes got these weird ideas into her head, said that twelve years old was too young for having real boyfriends. It didn't matter that simply loads of people who were twelve years old had been having real boyfriends ever since they were eleven, and that Jo knew that for a fact; Mrs Jameson said they didn't, and that was that.

But in any case, according to Barge, who was an expert on the subject (Barge was an expert on virtually any subject you cared to mention) real boyfriends smacked horrible wet kisses on your lips and got you into dark corners and slobbered over you, and since Jo didn't have any real desire either to be got into a dark corner and slobbered over *or* to have wet kisses smacked on her lips, she had been quite happy to keep the relationship sort-of. She still was, except, there was no denying it, a relationship which was only sort-of did begin to pall after a while. She had to admit that Robbie no longer seemed anywhere near as important in her life as he had, say, at the end of last term, or even a couple of weeks ago when they had gone swimming together. In fact, the thought of going to the Club and seeing him there, all beaming and blushing and eager to please, was just the tiniest bit – well – *boring*.

'You going to come or not?' said Matty. 'You might just as well. Practise any more you'll go cross-eyed. Anyway, it'll be too dark soon.'

'Oh, all right.' Who cared if she was still wearing her school skirt and blouse? It was only Robbie.

Robbie was there, waiting for her. His face brightened as he saw her. He came lolloping across, all beaming and bashful, just as Jo had known he would. It wasn't fair to feel irritated. After all, he wasn't doing anything wrong.

Robbie said, 'Hallo!'

'Hi,' said Jo, playing it cool.

'Hi,' said Matty, playing it even cooler.

'How's school?' said Robbie.

'It's OK,' said Jo.

'It's OK,' said Matty.

Robbie attempted a joke: 'Been made chief slave driver again?'

'No, *thank* you,' said Jo. 'Once was more than enough.'

'Dead right,' said Matty. 'Right bossy cow you were.'

'Well, you would all play up all the time.'

''Course we did! It was what we voted you in for, wasn't it?'

'She can't keep order for toffee,' said Tom.

'I'm sure she *could*,' said Robbie.

'Well, she didn't!' Matty cackled and went loping off across the room to join Jool and Nadge.

'What about you?' said Jo, making an effort. It was mean to be nasty to someone just because suddenly, for no reason, you seemed to have gone off them. 'I s'ppose you've been voted boss again?'

'He's always boss,' said Tom.

'Like Gerry. It's a pity she doesn't live near enough to come to the Club. You and Gerry'd get on.'

Robbie looked hurt. Jo knew that what he would have liked to say was, 'You and I get on!' but that he couldn't because of Tom being there.

'She's into netball.' Tom jerked his head at Jo. 'She's got all mad and besotted.'

'I haven't got all mad and besotted!'

'I call it mad and besotted,' said Tom. 'Spending every evening chucking balls into a net.'

'I'm *practising*,' said Jo.

'You need to practise,' said Robbie, 'if you want to be any good.'

'She's got a special reason,' said Tom. 'Haven't you?' He leered at Jo. 'Do you want me to tell him what it is?'

'You shut up!' said Jo.

Tom adopted a threatening posture, arms raised for a karate chop. 'Don't you tell me to shut up!'

'Shut up!' shrilled Jo. 'Shut up, shut up!'

'You looking for trouble?' said Tom. He advanced upon her: Jo backed away.

'You hit me and I'll bash you!'

'I'd like to see you try!' scoffed Tom, though in fact Jo had bashed him on several occasions and had once even made his nose bleed.

Robbie, alarmed, pushed himself between them. (Robbie had a sister called Jenny whom he would never have dreamed of fighting. He didn't understand the dynamics of a real tooth-and-claw relationship.)

'Fight to the death!' roared Tom. 'No holds barred!'

Tom was just showing off. Jo decided to show off with him. (She could tell that it was shocking Robbie.) She ran at Tom and kicked him. Tom grabbed Jo's arm and twisted it behind her back. Jo lashed out. Tom howled. Robbie ran forward.

'Look, honestly,' he said, 'if Jo's got a secret, I don't want to hear it.'

They stopped and looked at him. What was he on about? What secret?

'Oh, *that*,' said Tom. Casually he let go of Jo's arm. 'It's not a secret any more, I shouldn't think . . . I should think the whole of her school knows about it by now. But I won't say anything *for the moment*. Not so long as she behaves herself,' he added.

Jo rubbed at her arm as she watched Tom go striding confidently off to join Nadge and the others at the table tennis table. (Last term Nadge had gone out with Tom. She must have been *loopy*.)

'Are you all right?' said Robbie. 'He didn't hurt you, did he?'

Considering it was Tom who had done all the howling, Jo thought that was a pretty daft question.

'Heavens!' she said. 'That's *nothing*. He pushed me into the wardrobe one time and broke the door.'

Robbie looked suitably horrified. 'What did your parents say?'

'Dad said, "They're at it again," and Mum said she didn't know what she'd done to be cursed with such ruddy rotten kids. And then she made us pay for a new wardrobe door.'

'*Both* of you? That doesn't sound very fair,' said Robbie.

'Well, I was the one who fell into it,' said Jo.

'Yes, but Tom was the one who pushed you.'

'Yes, but only because I bit him.' She hadn't really bitten him (she had *tried* to bite him) but she was having fun watching Robbie's eyes grow rounder and rounder. 'I bit him and I pulled his hair out by the roots.'

'I see.' Robbie looked at her, doubtfully. 'He must have done something to upset you.'

'I expect so,' said Jo. 'He usually does. He is a most annoying sort of boy. But then I think most boys are annoying, don't you? Until they get to be about sixteen. Then they're not so bad.'

'Am I annoying?' said Robbie.

Jo felt a strong temptation to say, 'Yes! You're

annoying me right at this very minute.' But it wouldn't have been kind, and anyway she would have found it difficult to say exactly *how* he was being annoying. He was only being Robbie, the same as he'd always been. She glanced rather wistfully across the room, to where a game of table tennis was in progress, Jool and Matty against Nadge by herself. Tom had picked up a bat and was trying to elbow himself in but Nadge wasn't letting him. Good! That was *good*. Tom got his own way far too often. She wished he and Robbie would go off somewhere together so that she could join in the game. She bet Nadge wouldn't object to her.

'Would you like me to get you a Coke?' said Robbie.

'We'll each get our own,' said Jo. She didn't mean to be ungracious but you had to pay your way or else you became beholden. It was important to keep your independence.

'Have you ever collected stamps?' asked Robbie, as they sat drinking their Cokes.

Jo blew down her straw to make bubbles. 'No,' she said. 'Why?'

'I just wondered,' said Robbie.

Silence. The table tennis was still going on. Tom had disappeared.

'Do you?' said Jo.

'Collect stamps?' said Robbie.

'Yes.'

'I did,' said Robbie. 'Once.'

Fascinating. Tom came back, pushing and jostling with a couple of other boys.

43

'I quite enjoyed it,' said Robbie. 'Getting to know all the different countries.'

'Sounds too much like geography,' said Jo. 'I can't stand geography.'

'But it's important,' said Robbie. 'Knowing where places are.'

'Mm . . . maybe.'

Jo sucked the last of her Coke, making busy slurping noises as the bottle emptied. She wished this were a structured evening, when Mrs Barlow organized them into playing games or doing quizzes or watching videos. She was getting really bored, just sitting here.

'Of course, you could always look them up in an atlas,' said Robbie, 'I suppose. But it's far better if you actually *know*. Then when they're talking about places, like on the news, you can picture them and know where they are in relation to other places. Like suppose they said Lithuania, for instance –'

'They'd show a picture of it probably. That's what they usually do.'

'Yes, but if they *didn't* –'

I shall scream in a minute, thought Jo. She sprang up. 'I'm just going over to have a word with Nadge.'

'I'll come with you,' said Robbie.

The evening dragged on. Jo began to wonder if perhaps she had grown out of the Youth Club. It was all right for Tom because even though he was older than she was, everyone knew that girls grew up faster than boys. There were times when Tom at thirteen and three-quarters behaved like a retarded ten-year-old. Robbie didn't; but then Robbie kept boring on about

44

stamp collecting and atlases. Jo almost felt that she would rather be lured into a dark corner and slobbered over than have to listen to someone talking about atlases. She *loathed* geography.

At the end of the evening they walked home in a threesome, Jo and Matty and Tom (Robbie lived in the opposite direction). As they left Matty at her front door Tom said fiercely to Jo, 'What's up with Nadge?'

'Nothing, as far as I know,' said Jo. 'Why?'

'She didn't want me to play table tennis with her.'

Jo shrugged. So what? *She* wouldn't want Tom playing table tennis with her. She didn't imagine anyone would. Tom was what her dad called 'a slasher and whammer'. He slashed and whammed quite indiscriminately, so that balls went all over the place – up to the ceiling, into the light bulb, out of the windows, on to the floor. You couldn't ever have a really proper game.

'She's ignoring me,' said Tom. (Good, thought Jo. Serve him right.) 'I kept trying to talk to her, and she wouldn't listen.'

'Maybe she's gone off men.'

Going off men seemed to be the fashion amongst the Eighth Years this term. Jo thought perhaps it had something to do with a supply teacher they had had for a short while in the summer. Her name was Ms Moston and she had been a bit potty, but she had also been a feminist and some of what she said had obviously sunk in.

'You've got to ask her for me,' said Tom.

'Ask her what?'

'Why she's gone off me.'

'I'm not going to ask her!'

'You'd better,' said Tom, 'unless you want me telling Robbie about You-Know-Who.'

Jo tossed her head. 'Think I care?'

'I will,' said Tom. 'I'll tell him.'

'So do it!' said Jo. She flounced into the house as her mum opened the door. '*Boys*!' said Jo.

4

The House netball trials were held on Monday, after school. Those taking part from 8N were the Laing Gang, the Bookends, Gerry Stubbs and Nadge. Jo, the Mouse and Bozzy, who were still only twelve, would definitely get places in the Under-13s; Jo and Bozzy just might be promoted to the Under-14s. But what Jo really wanted was to be selected to go forward for one of the school teams. That was where glory ultimately lay. That was when Sarah would really sit up and take notice.

'That Jo Jameson . . . she's going to be a topnotch player one of these days. I shouldn't be at all surprised if she were to end up playing for the county.'

She wouldn't, of course; it was all a pipe dream. It was Nadge who was going to end up playing for the county, and Nadge who was going to grab all Sarah's attention. Not that Nadge would do it deliberately; she just couldn't help it. She was like a jet-propelled jumping bean on a netball court.

For trial purposes, Nadge and Jo were both playing centre, opposite each other. Try as she might, there was no way Jo could manage to keep up with Nadge and her quicksilver leapings and dancings about the court. She felt depressed as they walked back into

47

school at the end of the trials. (Nadge's team had won easily, by twenty goals to eleven.)

'Relax, Jo!' Sarah squeezed her arm, bracingly, in passing. 'Don't look so downcast . . . remember, all the heavyweights were on the other side!'

When she said heavyweights, she meant all the best players . . . Nadge and Fij, and the crew from the year above, Katy Wells and Jan Hammond and their mob. Jo probably wouldn't even get a place in the House Under-14s, never mind be chosen for the school.

'Hey!' Fij was nudging her excitedly with her elbow. '*She touched you*!'

I don't want to be touched, thought Jo; I want to be noticed, I want to be important, I want to be Someone! Nadge was someone. As form games captain she attended all the House games meetings. As a member of the school Under-14s, which she was bound to be, she would go on coach journeys to other schools and stay to eat school teas. And Sarah would be there, sitting on the same coach, eating the same tea, and even if she didn't actually lower herself to communicate with Nadge, which could, after all, hardly be expected, she would at any rate be aware of her as a presence.

'If I had a pash on somebody –' the Gang had taken to the word *pash*; it creased them every time they said it. 'If I had a pash,' said Fij, when the giggles had subsided and she was able to speak again, 'I'd be in *ecstasy*!'

'I haven't *got* a pash!' How many more times did she have to tell them? You could admire a person and want to be noticed by them without all this sloppy nonsense.

48

'Does your arm burn?' said Fij. 'Have you got stigmata?'

'Tomatoes?' That was Bozzy, eavesdropping on other people's conversations and getting hold of totally the wrong end of the stick, as usual. 'Where's she got tomatoes?'

'On her arm.'

'On her *arm*?'

Fij, overtaken by yet another fit of the giggles, spluttered: 'She was *touched*.'

'Well, I know she's *touched*,' said Bozzy.

'Off the wall,' said Barge.

'It's all this passion . . . it's driving her barmy.'

'No, no!' screamed Fij, so that everybody within a twenty-mile radius (which included Sarah) could hear. 'She was touched by *Her*.'

'Oh! By *Her*.'

'The Divinity!'

'*Touched* –'

'On the *arm* –'

'On the bare *flesh* –'

'Oooooooooooooh!' howled Bozzy. 'It gives me the shivers just to think of it!'

'What's all the noise about?' Sarah had come marching back down the corridor. 'Why are you all hooting and yelling like a load of screech owls?'

Barge, Bozzy and Fij instantly collapsed. Jo felt like crawling under the nearest chair and gnawing her way through the floor boards.

'Just stop it,' said Sarah, 'and act your age. For goodness sake!'

49

Sarah went off again. Gerry Stubbs, neatly sidestepping the three prostrate gigglers, said, 'Honestly! You people! You are supposed to be Second Years.'

'Eighth,' muttered Jo; but who ever took any notice of her?

That evening, after tea, Robbie rang up, eager to hear how the trials had gone. Jo said irritably, 'I don't know yet. They don't tell you on the *spot*.'

It was hateful to be cross with someone who was only trying to show an interest, but it was the way she was feeling. She couldn't help it. Well, she supposed she *could* help it, if she wanted; but she wasn't sure that she did want. It did you good, sometimes, to lash out at someone.

'So when do you think they'll let you know?' said Robbie.

'Don't ask me,' said Jo.

Robbie hesitated. 'I'll give you a ring tomorrow. Shall I?'

'If you want,' said Jo.

'I'll keep my fingers crossed for you.'

'Bit late for that,' muttered Jo, as she bumped the receiver back down.

Next morning, during break, they went to look at the notice board. Nadge, who was not yet quite thirteen, had bypassed the Under-14s and been put straight into the second team, along with great galumphing creatures from Years 10 and 11. She had also been selected to play for the school, the only person of their year who had. Even for the school she had bypassed the lowest of the low and was playing with people older than herself.

Barge, Fij and Jo, along with Bookend Emma, were in the House Under-14s, with Gerry as reserve; Bozzy and the Mouse stayed in the Under-13s, with Bozzy as captain. Bozzy, at least, was happy.

'Me, captain!' She couldn't get over it.

'Whatever will they think of next?' marvelled Barge.

'Well, but Sarah has obviously had the wit to realize, *at last*, that just because I am somewhat on the small side does not mean,' said Bozzy, inflating herself like a puffball, 'that I am a nincompump.'

'Poop,' said Barge.

'Pardon?' said Bozzy.

'I said *poop*,' said Barge. 'Poop, poop, poop!'

'I don't see there's any need to be rude,' said Bozzy, 'just because you haven't been made captain.'

Barge rolled her eyes and tapped a finger to her head.

Jo said: 'How has Sarah realized?'

'Realized what?'

'That you are not a nincompoop.'

'She has seen me,' said Bozzy, 'on a horse.'

'Well, *I*'ve seen you on a horse,' said Barge. 'I've also seen you *off* a horse – diving headfirst towards the ground. I thought at the time,' confided Barge, 'how fortunate it was that her head happened to be empty. . . . For a person with a brain, it could have been disastrous.'

'That was months ago,' said Bozzy, aggrieved. 'I don't come off at all, hardly, these days. Sarah said

51

only last week that I was doing very nicely. Those were her exact words . . . *very nicely*. So there.'

'Why did she say that?' said Jo.

'Because I am doing very nicely!'

'Yes, but how does Sarah know?'

'Oh! Didn't I tell you?' said Bozzy. 'She rides at the same stables.'

Bozzy went prancing off ahead, making clicking noises with her tongue. Jealousy roared and raged within Jo's breast.

'Captain!' said Barge. 'She must be out of her mind. She should have kept Jammy back and used her.'

'But she wanted Jam for the Under-14s.'

'Under-14s, Under-13s, where's the difference? Oy! Dobbin!'

With a loud whinnying noise, Barge went cantering off after Bozzy. Fij and Jo strolled on for a while, in silence. After a bit, Fij said: 'There *is* a difference. She wouldn't have moved you up a team if she didn't think you were good enough.'

Jo humped a shoulder, refusing to be consoled. She might be just a little better than Bozzy or the Mouse, but she wasn't as good as Nadge. *She* hadn't been whizzed up to the second team. *She* hadn't been selected for the school. And to think that Bozzy, little, plaited, pop-eyed Bozzy, actually met Sarah socially, on a horse!

That afternoon, Jo raced home from school not to practise netball – for what was the point, *now*? – but to corner her mother in the kitchen before Tom could arrive and spoil everything.

'Do you think,' said Jo, breathlessly, 'that I could have riding lessons?'

'Do you think,' said her mother, 'that I could have a netball? Do you think that I could have some ice skates? Do you think that I could have a mouth organ? Do you think that I could learn ballet? Do you think,' said Mrs Jameson, 'that we are made of money?'

'Well, no, of course not. Not *made* of it,' said Jo. But they had bank accounts, didn't they? And bits in the building society? And bits in pots around the house? 'The thing *is* –' said Jo.

'The thing *is*,' said Mrs Jameson.

Jo looked at her, reproachfully.

'All right, go on!' said Mrs Jameson. 'You tell me what your thing is, then I'll tell you mine.'

'The thing is,' said Jo, 'that I would very much *like* to have riding lessons as I feel I should be good at it and I find the horse a noble animal. And if I'm going to have them, then I need to start having them soon, before I am thirteen, for instance, on account of your bones getting set and if you leave it too late it's difficult to learn.

'Also,' said Jo, 'riding is a good outdoor hobby which would take me into the fresh air and out from under your feet and bring untold benefits, e.g. meeting lots of people, e.g. giving me a healthy complexion, e.g. being good for one's posture, e.g. being a social skill, e.g. being another string to one's bow should one ever decide to become, for example, an actress –'

'Is one ever likely to become, for example, an actress?' said Mrs Jameson.

'Well, you never know,' said Jo.

'How true!' said her mother.

Jo frowned. This wasn't going at all as she had planned.

'Melanie Peach,' she said, 'who is a girl in our class who has an uncle who is an actor and who as a matter of fact is acting right now in a famous TV soap called "Lovat Lane" that you never watch because you scorn such things, but millions and millions *do*, is going to become an actress herself and *she* says,' said Jo, 'that the more things you can do the better, e.g. singing –'

'Which you manifestly *cannot* do.'

' – e.g. dancing, riding, fencing, driving,' gabbled Jo.

'Eating fire?' suggested Mrs Jameson.

'*Any*thing,' said Jo.

'In that case, just for the meanwhile, why don't you concentrate your efforts on learning how to add two and two together and make them come to four? I should think,' said Mrs Jameson, 'that that would be a pretty useful accomplishment for anyone, whatever they wanted to be.'

'You're not taking this seriously!' cried Jo.

'I am, I promise you! But *my* thing, which is admittedly a good deal simpler than your thing, is the unarguable fact that your father and I do not happen to be millionaires.'

'Neither are Bozzy's mum and dad, and she's doing it!'

'Maybe Bozzy hasn't already demanded ice skates and mouth organs and ballet shoes and –'

'But I didn't get any of them!'

'You got your netball.'

'Yes, but I didn't get any of the others!'

'That was because by the time the deadline came round you'd gone off the idea and didn't want them any more. Which is precisely,' said Mrs Jameson, thrusting a handful of cutlery at Jo, 'why I shall say to you now what I have said before . . . if you still want to do it by Christmas –'

'Christmas will be too late!' wailed Jo. 'I want to do it *now*!'

'Well, I'm afraid you can't. Life isn't like that . . . it's jam tomorrow, jam yesterday, but never jam today. That is the rule.'

Jo blinked. 'I beg your pardon?'

'*Alice Through the Looking Glass*,' said Mrs Jameson.

What had *Alice Through the Looking Glass* to do with it?

'I know it's unfair,' said Mrs Jameson, 'but it's the same for all of us – well, for most of us. Very few people ever get to have jam today. And let's face it, by Christmas you'll be into skittles or scuba diving. Just lay the table for me, there's a good girl.'

'Why me?' grumbled Jo. 'Why not him?'

'Because you're here and he's not, if you're referring to your brother. Stop sulking!'

It was enough to make one sulk. She bet Sarah's mother wasn't like this.

Robbie rang at eight o'clock. Jo said, 'Tell him I'm out.'

'Certainly not,' said Mrs Jameson. 'That's no way to treat people.'

'I'll tell him!' said Tom. He shot to his feet. 'I'll tell him you said to say that you were out 'cause you didn't want to speak to him!'

Jo just managed to beat him to the telephone. Robbie, of course, thought it was the eighth wonder of the world, Jo being in the Under-14s when she still had another six months to go before she was even thirteen. She didn't bother explaining to him that being in a House team wasn't enough; that what she wanted was to travel on coaches with Sarah Bigg and eat cream teas sitting opposite and be *noticed*.

Jo lay awake half the night, thinking up schemes by which she could bring herself to Sarah's attention. Riding was obviously out of the question; her mother was as stingy as could be when it came to parting with money. She didn't seem to mind shelling out hundreds and *hundreds* for someone to come and paint the front of the house a different colour – why bother, when it had been the same pea green for as long as Jo could remember? Why mess about with it? It had been perfectly all right, apart from the odd few cracks and a bit of flaking. Ask her for some trivial little thing like a pair of ice skates and it was 'We're not made of money, you know.' Wouldn't even open her purse the merest *crack* to give her only daughter what other people's daughters had as a matter of course. What with Claire learning ballet, Melanie taking drama courses – *Bozzy going riding*. Even Matty's mum and dad, who also weren't made of money, had bought Matty a camera

56

for her birthday. She bet a camera had cost loads more than a mouldy netball.

If Jo ever had children, she would let them try absolutely everything they wanted. How could you be expected to find out what you were good at if you weren't even allowed to try?

Meanwhile, there was still the problem of Sarah. She knew that Jo *existed*, but what was the use of that? Michelle Wandres also knew that she existed. What Jo needed was the chance to identify herself – the chance to stand out from the crowd. To perform some act of heroism, perhaps, such as saving Sarah's life – or Sarah could perform some act of heroism and save Jo's life. Either way had possibilities.

Jo curled her toes in anticipation, as she rolled herself into a nice cosy ball in her duvet. Suppose . . . suppose, one day, she just happened to be walking over Petersham Common and saw a big black horse come galloping towards her out of control, with Sarah clinging terrified to the reins and –

No! Sarah wouldn't cling terrified, she would – she would have a broken arm, flapping uselessly at her side. She would have been riding through the woods and some idiot would have fired an airgun and frightened her horse so that the horse bolted, crushing Sarah's arm against a tree as it did so. Sarah would be in direst, ghastly agony, fighting off the waves of nausea, trying not to pass out, and Jo, heedless of her own safety, would go charging forward and hurl herself at the horse's head, grabbing hold of the bridle – would it be the bridle? She didn't know much about horses.

Anyway, whatever it was, she would grab hold of it, being pulled along the ground but pluckily hanging on, getting her hands skinned almost raw in the process, until she had the animal under control. Ignoring her own wounds she would help Sarah to dismount and support her as they stumbled off to get help. They would be taken by ambulance to the hospital, where Sarah's arm would be put in plaster and Jo's poor bleeding hands bathed and bandaged, and everyone would exclaim at her bravery and Sarah would declare that Jo had saved her life – as indeed she would have done.

It was a nice idea. The only trouble was, it wasn't very *likely*. How often did you come across people with broken arms sitting on top of horses bolting across Petersham Common?

Think of something else.

She could always go to the local baths and rescue Sarah from drowning – except that Sarah was probably a champion swimmer, whereas Jo could only manage a rather ineffectual breaststroke.

Maybe Sarah could come to the baths and rescue Jo from drowning? But did Sarah ever go to the baths, and if so, when? It was a great pity they didn't have a swimming pool at Peter's. If they had, Jo could have arranged to fall in and start drowning just as Sarah happened to be passing – taking it on trust, of course, that Sarah could swim.

Well, but anyway, they didn't have a swimming pool, so that was that out the way.

Bicycle accident outside Sarah's house? (N.B. *Find*

58

out where Sarah lives.) Fainting fit ditto? Fainting fit in *school*?

Jo was just in the process of crumpling herself tastefully at Sarah's feet at the bottom of the main staircase, causing Sarah to cry 'Jo!' in tones of anguish and come racing towards her, when most inconveniently she fell asleep. In her sleep, however, she dreamed that she was playing netball for the first team and saved the day by scoring the winning goal, so that was all right – though why she should be scoring goals when she was playing centre was never quite made clear. But then in dreams these things didn't matter. It was enough that Sarah should shake her by the hand and say, 'Jo, I thank you from the bottom of my heart. . . . Without you we should have been lost!'

The only problem with dreams was that sooner or later your mother started yelling at you up the stairs in a rage because she'd yelled at you three times already and did you want to be late for school because if so you were going the right way about it? And then you were forced into the realization that it *had* only been a dream and that you were still an abject nobody and that Nadge was playing for the school while you were only playing for the rotten Under-14s for the House and as far as Sarah was concerned you were simply one out of teeming millions, or at any rate dozens, and why why *why* couldn't you just for once do something to distinguish yourself?

5

'Quick!'
   'Quick quick!'
   'Quick!'
   'What –'
   'Hurry!'
   'Quick!'
   'Now!'
   '*Come*!'
   'What are you *doing*?' cried Jo. One minute she had been sitting quite quietly at her desk, happily re-arranging the contents so that they were in some kind of order instead of all mixed up higgledy-piggledy in a squalid mess; the next she found herself being viciously attacked by three screaming maniacs, all intent on grabbing at various portions of her anatomy and dragging her across the room.

   'Stop it!' yelled Jo, ricocheting off the back of some-one's chair and crashing into the sharp edge of someone else's desk and banging her head rather hard against the doorpost. 'Let me go, you idiots!'

   'Hurry!' panted Fij.

   'Quick!' giggled Bozzy.

   'Before it's too late!' With a final heave, Barge yanked Jo through the doorway. Attached like leeches

– Barge on one arm, Bozzy and Fij on the other – they hustled her along the corridor.

'*There!*'

Triumphantly, at the head of the stairs, they thundered to a halt. It was the purest misfortune, as Bozzy afterwards claimed, that Jo did not thunder to a halt with them.

'How were we to know you were going to go on moving?'

'And headfirst, too,' marvelled Barge. 'It's hardly what I should call a normal way for a person to go downstairs.'

'Especially,' added Fij, 'when someone else is on the way up.'

The someone else was Sarah, with an armful of books. *Wham!* like a bullet went Jo's head, somewhere in the region of Sarah's midriff. Sarah, dropping her books, went plummeting backwards into the arms of Michelle Wandres. Michelle (always so *clumsy*, grumbled Bozzy) lost her footing and crashed into Jasmine Patel on the step below. Jasmine, knocked off balance, cannoned into a Seventh Year, who promptly squealed like a pig and fell over. Books went flying everywhere.

'Honestly! What is the matter with you people?' Jasmine glared angrily up the stairs at Barge & Co. clustered at the top and Jo hanging drunkenly to the banisters a few steps down. 'Can't you learn to grow up and behave like civilized human beings? You're like a load of football hooligans!'

Jo, red-faced and cringing, fell to her knees and

scrabbled blindly amongst the forest of legs, trying to locate the scattered books.

'Do you mind?' snapped Michelle. 'I can do without my legs being pawed at!'

'Just get to your feet, Jo, for goodness sake!' That was Sarah, in tones of somewhat weary exasperation. 'Take yourselves back to your classroom, or wherever you're meant to be, and stop cluttering the place up.'

'Yes, and you can come along to the Prefects' Room at the start of break and bring the order mark book with you – all of you! I'm just about sick of the way you lot carry on. I've already warned you,' said Michelle, eyes glinting evilly at them behind her glasses, 'I don't intend to put up with a repetition of what we had last term. Perhaps this will show you that I mean business!'

'That,' gasped Fij, as they regained the safety of their own classroom and collapsed, panting, behind their desks, 'is the most ill-tempered thing I ever heard!'

'*No* sense of humour,' fumed Barge. (Having none herself, she was always indignant at the lack of it in others.)

'Wouldn't you think,' huffed Bozzy, 'that they could have seen the funny side of it?'

'What funny side?' Jo said it sourly. She certainly couldn't see anything funny about being made to look an idiot in front of Sarah.

'Well,' gurgled Bozzy, 'you catapulting down the stairs and butting Sarah in the stomach –'

'And Sarah falling on top of Michelle –'

62

'And Michelle falling on top of Jasmine –'

'And Jasmine falling on top of that Seventh Year –'

'Who nearly got *crushed*!'

The three of them creased.

'Laugh?' gasped Barge. 'I haven't seen anything so funny in years!'

'Like a pack of *cards* –'

'One after another –'

'All fall down!'

Jo watched in distaste as Fij rolled about in a hoop and Barge and Bozzy collapsed helplessly on each other's shoulders.

'Well, thank you,' said Jo, banging down her desk lid. 'Thank you all *very* much. I just hope you're satisfied . . . you cretins!'

They stopped laughing and looked at her, hurt.

'What is she going on about?' said Bozzy.

'Just because it went a teensy bit wrong . . . ' said Barge.

'We meant well,' said Fij. 'We thought you'd be pleased to see Sarah.'

'We were under the impression,' said Bozzy, 'that we were doing you a favour.'

'Bringing you to her notice,' said Barge. 'Which I would have thought –' Barge gave one of her short, sarcastic barks – 'I would have *thought*, though of course you may correct me if I am wrong, was what a person would desire above all else when a person had a pash upon a person.'

'Pash!' simpered Bozzy.

Barge looked at her with cold disfavour. 'Not now,

dear,' she said. Bozzy was never one for knowing when
the moment was wrong.

'Some people,' said Fij, 'don't deserve people doing
them favours.'

Some people, thought Jo, ought to give up trying, if
that was the best they could do. It was one thing to
fantasize about gently crumpling up at a person's feet;
quite another to be clumsily hurled down the stairs on
top of them. She tried not to sulk, but it wasn't easy –
especially when Sarah opened the door of the prefects'
room, in answer to Barge's loud hammering, and said,
'I might have known it was you lot! Can't you do
anything without shattering people's eardrums? Jo, by
the way, I'd like a word with you when you've finished
your business with Michelle. I'll be over on number
one netball court. Come and find me.'

'*For hooliganism on main staircase,*' wrote Michelle,
in her cross spiky handwriting in the order mark book.
'And you can think yourselves lucky I'm only giving
you one apiece. You won't get off so lightly next time,
I can tell you!'

'So what's an order mark?' said Bozzy, grandly, as
they traipsed out into the playground. 'Just a blob on
a bit of paper . . . doesn't *mean* anything.'

'Until you get a whole page full of blobs and are
sent for by Stanny. And if Sarah is going to give me
another, *personal* one for being chucked down the
stairs on top of her,' said Jo, 'that means I shall have
more than any of you and it's *not fair!*'

Sarah was on number one court supervising a load

of Seventh Years. As Jo slunk up she said, 'Ah, there you are!'

Jo opened her mouth. 'I'm sorry I fell on top of you but it wasn't my fault, I was p– '

'Never mind all that!' Sarah brushed it aside, impatiently. 'Matty McShane tells me you're a good shooter.'

'Me?' Jo blinked.

'Well, unless I've got your name wrong . . . you are Joanne Jameson, aren't you?'

'Yes,' said Jo.

'So are you a good shooter? Or aren't you?'

'Um – well,' said Jo.

'Give it a go!' Sarah tossed a netball at her. 'Let's see what you can do.'

Bemused, in front of all the gawping Seventh Years, Jo took aim at the net. Her first three tries went bouncing off the rim.

'Relax!' murmured Sarah. 'Pretend you're in your back garden at home . . . that's where you do all your practising, isn't it?'

Jo wiped her hand down the back of her skirt and tried again.

'That's better! That's much better! Oh, that's splendid! Why ever didn't you put your name down for shooter at the trials?'

'Didn't think,' said Jo.

'Well, now, look, the school Under-13s are desperate for someone. I asked your friend Matty, because I knew she played for the House last year, but she said she's too busy going in for some photography competition. She said you were better than she was, anyway. So how about it? Do you want to hop along tomorrow lunch hour for a trial game? Give it a go?'

'Yes, *please*,' said Jo.

'OK, I'll tell Jayne – Miss Duncan. I'm not guaranteeing you'll get in, of course, but it would be nice if you could. We haven't a single person from Nellie's in the Under-13s.'

Jo walked on air for the rest of the day.

'You see?' said Bozzy. 'I told you we were doing you a good turn!'

'I haven't got in yet,' said Jo.

'No, but at least she thought of you.'

It had been Matty, actually. Matty was the person who had done her a good turn if anyone had.

'Don't mention it,' said Matty, as Jo tried to thank her on the way home. 'I just hope you get in, if that's what you want.'

It was what she wanted; more than anything in the world. She practised for two hours in the garden that evening, until the light had gone and it was too dark to see.

The trial game took place on number four court, tucked away in a corner behind the science block, all nice and private. Jo scored ten goals, and missed on three. Miss Duncan promised the team would be on the board, for next week's match against St Anne's, no later than Friday. Barge & Co., who had come along to watch and to cheer her on, assured Jo that if she didn't get in they would eat their hats, a strange expression much beloved of Mrs Stanley – 'If Jo gets more than two per cent, I'll eat my hat!' It seemed singularly meaningless used by people who to Jo's certain knowledge didn't have any hats, but she took it as being supportive and couldn't help feeling, herself, that she had done rather well. Her only sorrow was that Sarah hadn't been there to witness her triumph. Miss Duncan was nice – very young and blonde, with her hair in plaits so that she looked almost like a Sixth Former, which according to Bozzy she still had been when Bozzy had started in the Homestead – but for all that, she wasn't Sarah.

Encouraged, however, for Sarah did at least now know who she was – Jo Jameson, shooter: not just 'the girl with the netball' or 'one of that mob' – Jo confidently set out on Wednesday morning to ingratiate herself still further.

For the next two days it was virtually impossible for Sarah to move without tripping over a winsomely beaming Jo lurking in dark corners or springing unexpectedly out of cupboards. Smiling foolishly, Jo stood at the ends of passages endlessly holding open doors that Sarah had no wish to go through. Bursting with good intentions, she rushed off to be of assistance when Sarah and Jasmine between them were quite competently manhandling a bench from one side of a netball court to the other, managing in the process to bark Jasmine's shin with one end of the bench and drop the other on Sarah's foot. ('Thank you *so* much, Jo,' said Sarah. 'What would we have done without you?') With a glad cry of, 'I'll put those away for you!' she seized possession of one netball, one referee's whistle and fourteen coloured girdles, which Sarah had just that moment brought out from the games cupboards, and went racing all the way back with them again before anyone could stop her. A self-important Katy Wells was dispatched in pursuit.

'Sarah says,' puffed Katy, 'that she is very pleased to see you taking exercise, but could we have our ball and our whistle and our girdles back if you think you've quite finished with them? We would rather like them,' said Katy, 'as we were on the point of using them.'

'Oh! Certainly. By all means,' said Jo. It didn't do to show that one was flustered. She had learnt from Barge the value of rising to the occasion. 'I was going to bring them back again anyway. I only took them to make quite sure that they were good ones. There are some in this cupboard,' said Jo, improvising wildly, 'that are simply not fit for use.'

'Really?' said Katy. She half smothered a yawn. It was a principle with the Ninth Years to take anything said by an Eighth Year with a liberal pinch of salt. (It was a principle with the Eighth Years never to lose face in front of a Ninth Year.)

'I have checked them,' said Jo. Graciously she snatched up a whistle and a netball and a bunch of girdles and bundled them into Katy's arms. 'I think you should find these satisfactory.'

'We would have had a better game,' said Katy, coming across Jo later in the day, 'if you could have given us a whistle that *worked*.'

It was rather disheartening, but nil desperando, or whatever the phrase was.

She printed it in thick, black, curly letters on the front cover of her rough book and enclosed it in a shield. NIL DESPERANDO . . . let that be her motto.

'Neil Desperado?' said Bozzy, misreading as usual. 'Who's Neil Desperado? Is he a pop star?'

Barge looked at the others and slowly shook her head. 'It's a Latin phrase, dear, used by those of us who have some degree of familiarity with the Latin tongue. Neil desperado . . . never despair.'

'I don't,' said Bozzy. 'I gave up despairing ages ago. What's it supposed to mean?'

Barge turned her eyes heavenwards. Fij and Jo giggled. Crisply, from the front of the room, came Gerry's voice: 'It doesn't mean anything. The phrase you're looking for is nil desperandum – used by those of us who have slightly *more* familiarity with the Latin tongue.'

This time, it was Bozzy who giggled.

'Personally,' confided Barge, in audible tones to those round about, 'I never feel the need to converse in foreign languages. It always seems to me a sign of gross inadequacy.'

'Yes, and besides –' Jo continued, comfortably, to cross-hatch her shield in green and purple – 'it all comes to the same thing in the end . . . it's what one *thinks* a thing means that matters.'

'Never was a truer word spoken,' said Barge.

6

First thing Friday morning, Jo was at the notice boards, eagerly scanning the notices.

'Neil desperado,' encouraged Bozzy, suddenly bobbing up like a glove puppet at her side. 'Did you get in?'

Jo felt like saying that she hadn't yet found out and that in any case she would rather make the discovery by herself, *if* Bozzy didn't mind. There was such a thing as being allowed to lick one's wounds in private. But both Barge and Bozzy were totally impervious to hints.

'Look!' Bozzy was pointing with a stubby finger. Jo looked. '*Shooter, J. Jameson* . . . that's you! I told you!' said Bozzy. 'I said neil desperado!'

Jo was too happy to point out that she had been the one who said it first – wasn't it the motto on the cover of her rough book?

'You're playing an away match,' said Bozzy, sticking her face close up to the notice board. 'Next Tuesday, against St Anne's Convent. All their matches are refereed by real *nuns*. And they give you absolutely scrummy cream teas afterwards.'

And she could sit opposite Sarah – or at any rate

near her – and travel across town in the same coach. Oh, bliss!

Sarah proved most elusive that day; almost as if she were avoiding Jo on purpose. Jo skulked round corners and hung about in shadows and at one point even stalked her along the Upper Corridor, only to lose her somewhere between the Senior Library and the Music Rooms. At lunch time she laid what she thought was a cunning ambush outside the Prefects' Common Room, hiding behind a six-foot-tall statue donated by an old girl (who had probably just wanted to get rid of it) and popping her head out every time the door opened. She was still there, alternately hiding and popping, when the bell rang for the start of afternoon school. *Where was Sarah?*

'Excuse me.' Jo sidled out from behind her statue and dimpled winningly at a prefect called Elinor Whitehead, a nondescript sort of person with mad messy hair hanging over her face like an old dish cloth. 'Do you know where Sarah is, please?'

'I might do,' said Elinor. 'And there again, I might not. It would all depend what you wanted her for. If you just want to make a nuisance of yourself –'

'I wanted to tell her something.'

'Why not tell me and I'll give her a message?'

Jo pulled awkwardly at one of the sleeves of her sweater, folding it over her fist like a snood.

'You'll ruin that sweater,' said Elinor. 'Do you want to give me a message for her or not?'

'No, it's all right, thank you!' gasped Jo. She turned and went racing off down the corridor. How mean

71

some prefects were! Elinor obviously knew perfectly well where Sarah was; she just didn't want to say. Too self-important by half. She needn't think Jo was entrusting *her* with any message.

It was only when she arrived back in 8N's classroom that she learned, to her extreme irritation, from Barge and the others, that Sarah had been over on the playing field the whole lunch hour, 'Doing *very odd* things with Jasmine.'

'What sort of odd things?'

'Flapping her arms about and jumping up and down and *swash*buckling.'

'Swashbuckling?'

'Marching to and fro,' said Barge, 'looking all butch and aggressive and brandishing sticks.'

'I think,' said Fij, 'they were pretending to have a sword fight.'

'How very odd!'

'That is what I said,' said Barge. '*Exceedingly* odd. When prefects start behaving like First Years, that is, I mean, Seventh Years, it means they are plotting.'

'Plotting what?'

'That,' said Barge, 'is the question.'

'Maybe you could ask her,' said Fij. 'Next time you are holding one of your intimate conversations, maybe you could just slip it in.'

'How?' said Jo.

'Oh! I don't know, but it should be quite easy, seeing as you are so intimate with her.'

'You could say, "Excuse me, Sarah, but my friends happened to notice you behaving rather oddly on the playing field with Jasmine and wondered if you were all right." Something on those lines,' said Barge. 'Cloaking it, you see, in a concern for her well-being rather than mere curiosity.'

'Which it is,' said Bozzy.

'Which it is,' agreed Barge. 'Although,' she added, 'I do find it pays to keep a close eye on what is going on in this establishment. I mean, for all we know, they could be plotting absolutely anything . . . they could be plotting to suppress us.'

'Or overthrow the staff.'

'Or rope us in for some ghastly end-of-term thingy for the good of the House.'

'So if you *could* manage to edge it into your next *conversazione*,' said Fij, 'it would be immensely useful.'

'I'll see what I can do,' said Jo, without having the least intention of doing anything at all. It was gratifying they should think her relationship with Sarah had progressed as far as having cosy conversations, but if she ever *did* manage to get her on her own for just five seconds, she certainly wasn't going to waste precious talking time interrogating her.

Coming out of school in a hurry at the end of the day, Sarah found a beaming Jo blithely stepping out in front of her.

'You again!' cried Sarah.

Sarah sidestepped: Jo sidestepped with her. There on the pavement they performed a small, intricate dance. Slow, slow, quick-quick, slow. One step to the left, two steps to the right. Relevé en arrière, bourré en

73

avant. March time, waltz time. *One* two three, *one* two three –

'What do you want?' cried Sarah.

'I got into the team!' said Jo.

'What team?'

'The Under-13s – as shooter.'

'Did you? Good. I'm very glad to hear it. Now, if you don't mind –'

One step to the right, two steps to the left.

'We're playing St Anne's on Tuesday. All their matches are refereed by nuns.'

'Yes, well, I suppose they would be, wouldn't they? Considering it's a convent.'

'Do you mind being refereed by nuns?'

'It really doesn't bother me one way or the other, especially since I shan't be there.'

'You won't be there?' Jo stepped backwards, abruptly, into the gutter.

'I won't be there. Come back on the pavement before you get knocked down!'

Jo hopped back up again. 'Why won't you be there?'

'I'm not playing for the school this term; only for the House. I've got too many other commitments.'

Jo's eyes widened alarmingly, till they looked like twin saucepan lids.

'So you won't be coming on the coach? Or staying to have tea?'

'I'm afraid not,' said Sarah.

'I see.' Jo's lower lip trembled slightly. She drooped.

'Cheer up!' said Sarah. 'There are other things in

life. You can do something for me, if you like. Would you like to?'

'Yes, please!' Jo dimpled, suddenly ecstatic again.

'Right, well, if you'd care to go up to the Prefects' Room and ask whoever is there if they could let you have a letter which I've left on top of my locker, and then if you could very kindly post it for me on your way home, I should be most grateful. Could you do that, do you think?'

Jo nodded vigorously, almost bouncing herself back into the gutter.

'It would be extremely helpful, because I am in a bit of a hurry. I took it out of my bag and then went and forgot it. *You* won't forget it, will you?'

'No!' Jo's head flew dizzily from side to side.

'Because it is very important,' said Sarah. 'I want it to get somewhere by Monday.'

'I'll get it *immediately*,' said Jo.

'And put it in a box on your way home.'

'I will! I promise!'

Jo flew as if on wings up to the Prefects' Common Room. Michelle Wandres was there. Sourly, and not a little suspiciously, she handed Jo the letter.

'You are quite sure Sarah wants you to have it?'

'She *said*,' said Jo. 'I've got to post it for her.'

'Well, just make sure that you do!' snapped Michelle.

Why did prefects always assume that just because you were some lower form of life you couldn't even be trusted to carry out the simplest of tasks?

Carefully, Jo slipped the letter down the side of her

bag. She would put it in the post box at the top of Shapcott Road.

On her way out of school Jo was waylaid by Nadge, who was on her way back from netball practice, and wanted to talk to her about the form team. Now that Jo was playing shooter for the school, did she think she ought to play shooter for the form, and if she played shooter for the form then who did she think should play goal attack instead of her?

Jo went back down to the cloakrooms to discuss the matter while Nadge changed and then walked with her up Shapcott Road to the bus stop.

It was growing quite late by then and the first two buses that came along were full. Jo decided to walk on, up to the High Street, where she had more choice. At the bus stop in the High Street she ran into a group of girls she had known at Juniors and who were now at Fallowfield, a large mixed comprehensive where Jo and Matty had at one time wished they could have gone. They debated the respective merits of the two schools while waiting for their buses. One of the girls, Joanne Walters, who had always been known as Big Jo (Jo had been Jo in the middle, because of there being three of them all with the same name) came on the bus as far as the bottom of King Street. She and Jo reminisced about Juniors and agreed that it all seemed a very long time ago.

By the time she arrived home, Jo had forgotten all about Sarah's letter.

It wasn't until Sunday afternoon, belatedly settling down to the weekend's homework, that she unpacked her bag and made the dreadful discovery. The letter fell out along with her French and History textbooks and lay there, accusingly, on her desk. Jo stared at it, horrified. How *could* she? After she had *promised*?

Panic-stricken, she snatched it up. She was about to go racing up the road with it – though even then it would be too late: Sarah had said it was to get somewhere by Monday – when her eye fell on the name on the front of the envelope: *John Jestico*. John Jestico was a Sixth Former at Tom and Andy's school. Jo had once seen him in their school play, acting the part of Hamlet. He was tall and blond and rather beautiful. It had to be the same person; there couldn't be two people with the name John Jestico.

If he hadn't lived so far away – right over the other side of town – she might have been able to bike it over to him. But it didn't matter, Andy could take it in with him tomorrow and give it to him at school. No, he couldn't. Bother! Jo had just remembered: Andy was going off on a boring Geography field trip at some hideous and ghastly hour like five o'clock in the morning. Well, Tom would have to do it. Tom was very disobliging at times but he could hardly object to just handing someone a letter.

Jo looked at it. The letter. Lying there, in front of her. Addressed to a boy. Blond beautiful John Jestico.

With a little sigh, she turned it over. Goodness! It wasn't sealed properly. The flap was gaping open. In her hurry, Sarah obviously hadn't licked it properly.

Jo picked it up, intending to stick it down. As she did so, the envelope somehow . . . *slipped*, and the contents somehow – well – came out. Of course it was very very wrong to read other people's private correspondence, and had it been a letter she most definitely would not have done, and even as it was she didn't exactly *mean* to, it was just that she couldn't help seeing that it was a birthday card, with a picture of an old-fashioned motor car on the front, and the card sort of fell open and inside it Sarah had written *To John with love from Sarah* with an arrow pointing to the bottom right-hand corner and the letters PTO. And Jo turned it over and read, *Peter has now met Alice . . . I'm really excited about it! I think it should work well – so long as we can get some convincing Boys!!!*

That was what came of reading other people's birthday cards: you couldn't make any sense of them. Who was Peter? Who was Alice? Why did they need convincing boys? Jo wasn't any wiser than she had been before.

That evening, when she had finished her homework, she took the envelope – properly sealed – downstairs for Tom.

'It's tremendously important,' she said. 'It's got to be given to him on Monday morning.'

'Why should I give it to him?' said Tom.

'Well, because he's at your school and it's easy for you, and anyway because I'm *asking* you,' said Jo.

'Don't see why I should do you any favours,' said Tom, 'seeing as you won't do me any.'

'When wouldn't I do you any?'

'When I asked you to ask Nadge why she'd gone off of me.'

Jo was silent a moment.

'Perhaps that was because you *ordered* me. Instead of asking me nicely.'

'All right,' said Tom. 'If I ask you nicely to ask Nadge why she's gone off of me, you can ask me nicely if I'll give this letter to John Jestico.'

'OK,' said Jo. 'I'm asking you nicely.'

'And I'm asking you nicely.'

There was a pause.

'Well? Is it a bargain?' said Tom.

Jo sighed. 'I suppose so.'

It was all her own fault for forgetting Sarah's letter.

7

On Tuesday morning, Sarah came up to Jo in the playground and said, 'Jo, did you post that letter I gave you?'

Jo turned scarlet. 'Yes,' she said.

'Oh.' Sarah sounded puzzled. 'All right, then. So long as you did.'

Jo wrestled for a moment with her conscience. She hadn't actually *posted* it, of course; but she had done the next best thing. In fact, delivering something by hand was probably better than sending it through the post, because there were times when the post could get delayed or even lost. On one occasion it had even been stolen, whole mailbags full.

'It's not that I doubt you,' said Sarah. 'I just wanted to make sure.'

'It's gone,' said Jo. At least that was the truth.

'OK! No problem.'

Sarah raised a hand, signalling end of conversation. She went strolling off towards the Hut.

'What was that all about?' said Fij, curiously.

'Oh! Just a favour I did for her.' Jo preferred not to talk about it. Only let Barge & Co. sense something was afoot and they would prod and poke and generally *niggle* until they teased the whole story out of her.

'Let's go and do some practising . . . I need to, if I'm going to play against St Anne's.'

'Did you speak to Nadge yet?' said Tom, that evening.

'Not yet,' said Jo. 'I haven't had a chance. Did you give John Jestico that letter?'

'Letter,' said Tom. There was a pause. 'Oh! Yes,' said Tom. 'The letter.'

'Did you give it to him?'

''Course I did,' said Tom. 'I keep *my* side of a bargain.'

'I'll talk to her tomorrow,' promised Jo. 'When we go to St Anne's.'

It wasn't easy, talking to Nadge. For one thing, Jo felt embarrassed by it, and for another, Nadge was a very difficult person to get on her own. On the coach she sat next to her best friend from York, Lee Powell, who was also in the Under-14s. Jo didn't like to ask her in front of Lee. There wasn't any chance during the actual matches, which were all played simultaneously on St Anne's four netball courts (in any case, Jo was far too busy scoring goals), and there wasn't any chance at tea because they all had to sit with their own teams, which meant Jo being stuck with the Under-13s.

On the coach on the way home everyone was singing and making a noise, with Nadge dancing up and down the aisle and sitting on people's laps and reducing everyone, even Miss Duncan, to giggles; and when they finally arrived back at Petersham and were disgorged outside the school gates, Nadge went racing off up

Shapcott Road with Lee, in quite the opposite direction from Jo.

I'll do it tomorrow, thought Jo. There wasn't any rush.

Fortunately Tom was always out on a Wednesday evening, having his extra English coaching. (Imagine! Almost fourteen years old and he'd never yet managed to read a full-length book. He could admittedly add numbers together and make them come to the right things, but where was the fun in that?)

'How did the match go?' asked Mrs Jameson. 'Did you win?'

'Yes. Easily. Seventeen-four.'

'Good heavens! A walkover. How many goals did you score?'

'Eight,' said Jo.

'Eight! That's not bad, is it? Considering you've never played shooter before.'

Miss Duncan had said the same thing. She had come up to Jo after the match and congratulated her. She had said, 'Well done, Jo! You're shaping up very well. Considering you've never played shooter before, that was excellent.'

'I'd have thought you'd be over the moon,' said Mrs Jameson.

'I am,' said Jo. She was over the moon; of course she was. But having Miss Duncan congratulate her wasn't the same as if it had been Sarah. What she wanted was for Sarah to come up (preferably in front of other people) and say, 'I hear you did great things, Jo! Splendid! I only wish I could have been there to see you. Next time I really must make an effort and come along.'

But how would Sarah know, unless the results were read out in morning assembly? Perhaps Miss Duncan would tell her.

'Your little Jo Jameson was quite a find . . . scored eight goals in her first match! She's going to be a real asset.'

At nine o'clock, Mrs Jameson went off in the car to fetch Tom.

'I think I'll go to bed now,' said Jo. 'I'm feeling rather tired. If Tom wants me –' she looked hard at her dad. Mr Jameson didn't always listen when his children spoke to him – 'if Tom wants me,' said Jo, very loudly and clearly, 'will you tell him I'm asleep?'

'You're asleep,' said her dad.

'*All night*,' said Jo.

'All night,' said Mr Jameson.

She didn't want to face Tom before she had to; the morning would be quite soon enough.

Luck was with her: in the morning, Tom overslept. By the time he came stumbling downstairs, hair on end, struggling into his sweater, Jo was on the point of leaving. As Tom clattered in at one door, Jo went hurtling out of the other.

'Did you speak to Nadge yet?' yelled Tom.

'Not yet, do it today, can't stop, got to meet Matty!'

Jo was round the side of the house, across the flowerbeds and ringing at Matty's front door with the speed of an Olympic sprinter.

When Jo and Matty got on the bus, they found Jool

83

on the top deck, which was convenient as it meant that Matty and Jool sat and talked together, leaving Jo free to sit by herself and dream. What she dreamt was that she was in the playground at break and Sarah came up to her in front of all the Gang – and probably the rest of 8N as well – and said, 'Jo, I had to come and tell you . . . we're moving you up to the second team with Nadia!'

Jo could hardly believe her eyes when Sarah actually did come up to her in the playground at break.

'*Again*!' hissed Fij, digging Jo in the ribs as Sarah made her way purposefully towards them through a crowd of screeching seventh years.

'Someone's in favour,' said Barge.

'Jo,' said Sarah, in a strange tight voice quite unlike her normal free-and-easy musical tones, 'could I have a word with you, please?'

Somehow, Jo just knew this wasn't going to be her dream come true.

'Come over here a minute,' said Sarah. On legs that had suddenly gone all wobbly, like pillars of jelly, Jo tottered after her. 'You know what this is about,' said Sarah, 'don't you?'

Jo swallowed. 'Um –'

'You do,' said Sarah, 'don't you?'

It would have been nice to think it was about scoring eight goals against St Anne's and being promoted to playing shooter for the second team, but Jo couldn't really pretend to herself that it was.

'I had a telephone call last night,' said Sarah, 'from my boyfriend. He said that he had just got the birthday

84

card I sent him . . . a whole day late! He said that a boy called Tom Jameson had given it to him.'

Tom! She would murder him!

'I take it,' said Sarah, still in her strange tight voice, 'that Tom Jameson is your brother?'

Jo nodded, miserably.

'So what happened?'

'I thought – I thought it would be better,' mumbled Jo. 'I thought if I posted it it might not get there.'

'Why shouldn't it have got there? It had a first-class stamp! You only had to put it in the box. You promised me! You gave me your word!'

Jo hung her head. 'I thought it might get lost. I thought if I gave it to Tom –'

There was a pause.

'What did you think if you gave it to Tom?'

'I thought that way it was bound to get there.'

'Well, it didn't! Or at any rate, not on time. You ought to know by now that you can't rely on brothers – they'd forget their heads if they weren't attached to their bodies.'

'I'm very sorry,' muttered Jo.

'So you ought to be! How would you like it if you had a boyfriend and he thought you'd forgotten his birthday? You wouldn't, would you?'

Jo shook her head, keeping her eyes fixed on the toes of her shoes.

'I'm sure you meant well,' said Sarah, coldly, 'but in future, if you agree to do things for someone, *do* them. I'm extremely disappointed in you – I thought you could be trusted!'

Sarah turned and swung off across the playground. Her back looked very stiff and straight. She would probably never talk to Jo again.

'What happened?'

'What did she want?'

'Was she pleased?'

'Did she congratulate you?'

Barge, Bozzy and Fij had come zooming over. They surrounded her greedily. Like a herd of hornets, thought Jo. *Buzz, buzz, buzz*. She felt like swatting at them.

'Give!' said Barge.

'Tell!' said Fij.

'Tell what?' Jo slapped crossly at Bozzy, who was breathing down her neck. 'There's nothing *to* tell.'

'You mean you just stood and stared at each other?'

'I distinctly saw her lips moving!' said Barge.

'We don't have *secrets*,' said Bozzy.

Jo remained stubbornly silent.

'We have ways of making people talk, you know,' said Barge.

'Thumbscrews!' said Bozzy.

'The rack,' said Fij.

'Sensory deprivation,' said Barge. 'That means putting a sack over your head or keeping you in a tank of water for twelve hours.'

Jo tossed her head. 'Try it!' she said.

'We could use my school bag!' said Bozzy, excitedly. 'If I took all the books out, we c– '

'Oh, shut up!' said Barge, tiring of the game. 'If she doesn't want to talk, then she doesn't want to talk.'

'There's no rule that says you have to,' said Fij.

'But we don't have secrets!' screamed Bozzy. 'We –'

'Oh, *shut up!*' said Barge.

The Gang, on the whole – even Bozzy, once she'd got the message – were surprisingly tactful. Despite being prey to vulgar curiosity, they none the less respected, as Barge put it, 'a person's right to silence'. The day was perfectly horrid even so. In Home Ec. Jo managed to jam one of the sewing machines, mangling a piece of material until it looked like half-chewed shredded wheat – Mrs Dyer marvelled at it: in twelve years of teaching, she said, she had never seen anything like it.

In Gym, later in the day, Jo stubbed her toe against a piece of equipment and bruised it; and in Maths, immediately afterwards, she discovered that in her hurry to flee the house before Tom could get at her she had left her Maths homework behind. Mrs Stanley, in one of her more vengeful moods, was particularly unpleasant about it. She said she was fed up with people making excuses and Jo could take an order mark.

It was her third order mark in two days. Michelle had slapped another one on her yesterday for sliding down the banisters on her stomach, with her head hanging over the edge (it had seemed like a good idea at the time) and Miss Lloyd, in one of her periodic frenzies, had dished out half a dozen at random when giggling had broken out in her English lesson.

'Stupid tiny little minds!' Miss Lloyd had snarled.

Jo had been specially indignant: she had only started

87

giggling because Fij had started giggling. Giggles, like measles, were catching, as Miss Lloyd must very well know.

Jo was not in the best of tempers when she arrived home at the end of the day. Tom came in as she was complaining bitterly to her mother about the unfairness of life – 'It wasn't me that started it!'

'No, but I expect it usually is,' said Mrs Jameson.

What was *that* supposed to mean?

'Have you spoken to Nadge?' demanded Tom.

'No, I have not!' snapped Jo. 'Why should I speak to Nadge when you didn't deliver my letter?'

'I did deliver your slimy letter!'

'*Yesterday*! You delivered it *yesterday*!'

'So what? I delivered it, didn't I?'

'You were meant to do it on Monday, you blithering blasted fool!'

'*Jo*!' said her mother.

'Don't you call me a blithering blasted fool, you sodding cheat!'

'*Tom*!'

'*I* haven't cheated!' shrieked Jo. 'You're the one that's cheated! You told me you'd done it – you lied!'

'So did you! You said you were going to talk to Nadge yesterday and you never did –'

'No, and I never will, now! You've ruined the whole of my life and I hate you!'

'Drop dead!' said Tom.

Mrs Jameson hammered on the kitchen table with her fist.

'*Will* you be quiet, the pair of you! Tom, if I ever

hear you use language like that again to your sister, or
to anyone else for that matter, there is going to be big
trouble. Do you understand me? Jo, go upstairs and
wash your face and stop being hysterical. I've had just
about enough of you both! We give you everything you
could possibly want, and this is the way you repay us.
You make me sick!'

Tom, scowling, stamped out into the garden. Jo fled
upstairs, sobbing. It was all so unfair! So unspeakably,
hideously unfair! They didn't give her everything she
wanted. They'd never let her learn ballet or have her
ice skates, they refused point-blank to let her learn
riding, Tom told lies and got away with it, while she
was yelled at for being hysterical, Sarah wasn't ever
going to talk to her again, and –

'Hey!' Andy grabbed hold of her as she reached
the landing and went blundering along it towards her
bedroom. 'What's up with you?'

'Tom has just ruined my life!' wept Jo.

'Again?' said Andy. 'How?'

'S-Sarah sent a b-birthday card to John J-Jestico and
I was g-going to p-post it only I gave it to T-Tom
instead and he f-forgot to d-deliver it!'

'Oh,' said Andy. 'So she knows John Jestico, does
she?'

'He's her b-boyfriend and it was his b-birthday!'

'I shouldn't bother weeping any tears on his behalf,'
said Andy.

'I'm n-not!' Jo dug her fist into her eyes. She was
weeping tears on her own behalf, not John Jestico's.
'W-why, anyway?'

89

'He gets all he wants, don't you worry.'

'Don't you l-like him?' said Jo.

'He's all right.'

'Are you still g-going to come and see Sarah p-play netball one day?'

'Don't see there's much point now,' said Andy. 'Not if she's going out with John Jestico.'

Andy turned and went shooting off, three steps at a time, down the stairs. Jo heard the sitting-room door slam behind him. She took out her handkerchief and blotted at her eyes. Surely Andy hadn't fancied Sarah for himself? He was a whole year younger! Sarah wouldn't go out with someone a whole year younger. And anyway, once she discovered he was Jo's brother she wouldn't touch him with a bargepole.

The tears came streaming back. Short of rescuing Sarah from the jaws of death, she didn't see how she was ever going to be in favour again. Tom was the most loathsome, evil brother it was possible to have.

8

On her way in to school on Thursday morning, Sarah
glimpsed the tail end of a frightened figure hastily scuttling out of her way, round the corner: it was Jo. Ten
minutes later, sitting in morning assembly amongst the
rest of the prefects at the side of the Hall, she heard
a busy scuffling coming from the ranks of 8N, somewhere at her feet. Glancing down, she saw that that
was also Jo, urgently scrambling to safety on the far
side of Margery Laing and Chloë Boswood, where,
presumably, she hoped not to be seen.

At first break, strolling in the playground with Jasmine, she caught sight of a face coyly beaming at her
from behind an oak tree: she looked again, and it was
gone.

'What was that?' said Jasmine.

'Just one of the crosses I have to bear,' said Sarah.

At lunch time, going to the games cupboard for some
equipment, she pushed aside a pile of fencing jackets
and a body fell out.

'Jo, this really is getting beyond a joke,' said Sarah.
'May I ask what you are doing, hiding in the games
cupboard in a pile of fencing jackets?'

Jo picked herself up. She dimpled, winsomely.

'Trying to keep out of your way,' she said. 'In case you didn't want to see me.'

'So if you're trying to keep out of my way,' said Sarah, 'why keep getting into it, in the first place?'

'Oh, well, you see, as to that,' burbled Jo, 'I – um – came into the games cupboard, as it were – as it was – into the jackets, as you might say, entirely by – well! Accident. So to speak. I was under the misapprehension,' babbled Jo, 'that I was on the floor above and was stepping into the – um – whatever is on the floor above.'

'The cleaning cupboard?' suggested Sarah.

'Yes! The cleaning cupboard. I thought I was stepping into the cleaning cupboard to fetch an – um – a –'

'Cleaning cloth?'

'Cleaning cloth. To clean something with. That was what I *thought* I was doing, only as it turned out,' gabbled Jo, 'I – er – wasn't.'

'Quite. You were waltzing into the games cupboard to hide from me in a pile of fencing jackets.'

'Well, but I didn't think you'd want to see me after what happened about the letter!' burst out Jo.

'I said all I had to say about the letter yesterday. There is such a thing,' said Sarah, 'as letting bygones be bygones. So I should be greatly obliged if for the future you would try to behave more like a normal human being and less like a brain-damaged woodlouse and stop all this skulking and scuttling and lurking in corners, because it is becoming very trying. Do I make myself clear?'

92

Jo said, 'Yes, Sarah.'

'I want no more hiding in fencing jackets.'

'No, Sarah.'

'Right. So what are you hanging around for?'

'I'm sorry, Sarah.'

Jo backed humbly out of the games cupboard, her face all pink and blotched with embarrassment. Relenting slightly, Sarah called after her: 'If you care to have a look on the notice board you might find something of interest to your lot.'

'Oh, *thank* you, Sarah!'

Jo gasped, gratefully, and went galloping off like an excited sheepdog down the corridor, hair flopping as she ran.

'Joanne Jameson!' (In the games cupboard, Sarah winced.) 'How many times have I told you, *no running in the corridor*? And what's happened to your hair? Why isn't it tied back? You know the rules! Are you looking for another order mark? Honestly,' snapped Michelle, 'some of you people never cease to astound me!'

Going at a fast trot – a trot could hardly be classed as *running* – Jo reached the notice board. Eagerly she scanned it. *Of interest to you lot* . . . Sarah had obviously meant the Gang. What would be of interest to the Gang?

A notice caught her eye – *Can you act? Can you dance? If so, read on! This concerns YOU.*

Jo zoomed in closer.

We are pleased to announce, said the notice, *that*

93

*the House end-of-term production will be PETER
MEETS ALICE AT THE MAD HATTER'S TEA
PARTY, an entertainment in one act devised by Sarah
Bigg and Jasmine Patel from the books by J. M.
Barrie and Lewis Carroll, to be directed by Jasmine
Patel.*

*The part of Peter will be played by Sarah Bigg, the
part of Alice by Tamsin Marshall.*

*Casting for the Mad Hatter, the March Hare, the
Dormouse, Lost boys & assorted Playing Cards will
take place on Monday at 3.30 p.m. in the Assembly
Hall. N.B. Playing Cards must be able to dance.*

Anyone interested, please sign below.

Jo couldn't wait. (So *that* was what the message in the
birthday card had referred to!) She whipped out her
pen and signed her name there and then, the very first
person to do so. It wasn't until she had gone leaping
back to the classroom (narrowly avoiding yet another
confrontation with Michelle Mealy Mouth Wandres)
that she remembered the Gang's embargo. What was
it Barge had said? *I wouldn't take part in another of
their childish productions if they went on their bending
knees and* begged *me!*

Oh, well! Jo gave a little defiant skip as she threw
open the door. That was just too bad. She wasn't going
to go and scratch her name out just to keep Barge
happy. They might be a Gang, but that didn't mean
they had to be clones. All the same, it might be as well
to tread carefully; Barge's wrath could be very terrible.

'Do you remember,' said Jo, leaning companionably

across Barge's desk, 'what you said at the beginning of term about the end-of-term production?'

'Yes,' said Barge. 'I said I wouldn't be in it if they went on their bending knees and begged me. Why?' An idea struck her. 'They're not *going* to beg me, are they?'

'They might be,' said Jo. 'They haven't actually said. But I expect they would very much *like* you to be in it.'

'I dare say they would,' said Barge. 'That is their problem. Do you mind not splodging all across my bilge book? I have just written in it in *real ink*.'

'Sorry,' said Jo.

'Why, anyway? What do you want to know about the end-of-term production for?'

'Well –' Jo fiddled with the pencils in Barge's pencil case. 'It's just that Sarah and Jasmine have devoured, I mean devised, this entertainment. It's called "Peter Meets Alice at the Mad Hatter's Tea Party", and it's all about Peter P –'

'Do you mind not messing with my pencils?' said Barge. 'I've just sharpened them.'

'Sorry. It's all about Peter Pan meeting Alice in Wonderland and Sarah is playing Peter and –'

'And you want to play Alice.'

'No, Tamsin Marshall's playing Alice.'

'Tamsin Marshall? Excuse me one moment,' said Barge. She hung her head into the gangway and made violent vomiting noises. Jo, as a matter of principle, followed suit.

Tamsin Marshall was in the year above them. She

had long yellow hair, which she wore in a big fat saus-
agey plait that came down to her waist and swung to
and fro as she walked like a misplaced elephant's trunk.
When she let it out of her plait it descended like a
shower curtain all about her face so that you couldn't
immediately tell which was the front of her head and
which was the back. But the really yucky thing about
her was that she belonged to Year 9. Year 9 and Year
8 were traditional sworn enemies.

'That's better,' said Barge, removing her head from
the gangway. 'So tell me –' she sat back, comfortably,
on her chair – 'what exactly is the problem?'

'Well, it's just that they're casting on Monday and
they're looking for Lost Boys –' boys were very important; Sarah had said so in her message on the birthday
card. *So long as we can get some convincing Boys.* 'I
thought I might try auditioning,' said Jo. 'For the
House, you know. For the *Cup*. And of course for the
form, what with Tamsin Marshall – yeeeurgh!' She
made a symbolic being-sick noise – 'Tamsin Marshall
being Alice, it seems only right that *one* of us should
be represented. I know what you said about last year
and us being made a laughing stock and all the rest,
but that *was* Wendy Armstrong and this *is* Jasmine
Patel. And of course Sarah. I am sure,' said Jo, earnestly, 'that Sarah wouldn't make us a laughing stock.
She really isn't at all that sort of person. So I've put
my name down but I thought I ought to tell you because
you did say that we shouldn't and –'

'Oh, my dear child!' Barge waved a patronizing paw.
'We quite appreciate that your situation has changed.

96

We were not to know then that you would be in the throes of a pash. Were we?'

'I'm thinking of the *House*,' said Jo.

'Of course you are.' Barge smiled, sweetly. Her tone was kind and soothing. 'There's no need to be embarrassed. We're your friends,' said Barge. 'We understand.'

There were times when Jo couldn't decide which was worse: Barge being bellicose or Barge being benevolent.

By the end of the day, when she went along to the notice board to sneak another quick look, she found that the only people from 8N to put their names down for auditions, apart from herself, were Melanie, Lol and Claire. She was just turning away when Nadge appeared, looking somewhat sheepish.

'Got a pen?' said Nadge.

Jo fished one out of her bag. She could hardly believe her eyes when Nadge used it to add her name to the list. Since when had Nadge been interested in acting?

'Wasn't my idea,' said Nadge. 'Sarah said to do it.'

'*Sarah*?' (Rage, rage! Jealousy and rage!)

'She just came up to me,' said Nadge. 'She said, "How'd you fancy the idea of being a lost boy?"' Nadge wrinkled her nose. 'I didn't even know what she was talking about. But she said to give it a go, so I s'ppose I'll have to. I dunno.' Nadge shrugged. 'Just s'long as I don't have to learn too many lines.'

'Did you tell that to Sarah?' said Jo. 'Did you tell her you don't want to have to learn too many lines?'

'Yes. I said I didn't like having to learn reams of

stuff 'cause we already have to do it for poetry and I didn't want to have to do any more.'

'What did she say?'

'She just laughed.'

'And she still wants you to audition?' In *spite* of Nadge not being willing to learn lines? It was almost unbelievable! The whole point of acting was that you should have lines.

'She seemed to think it'd be all right,' said Nadge, vaguely. 'She just said to come along and we'd sort things out at the time.'

She was making it sound almost as if a part had already been offered her. Why would Sarah want Nadge? It wasn't even as if she could act! Jo jealously revolved it in her mind on the way home. It could only be, she decided, because Nadge looked boyish. Jo decided there and then that she would look boyish, too.

'Do you think –' she crashed through the back door without even bothering to check whether Tom was there. Fortunately he wasn't. 'Do you think that I could have my hair cut? *Immediately*?'

'No,' said Mrs Jameson. 'Why?'

'It is *absolutely imperative*,' said Jo.

Her mother cocked an eyebrow. 'Suddenly discovered you've got nits?'

'Don't be disgusting!' screeched Jo. 'That's foul!'

'So what's so imperative about it?'

'I need it for the end-of-term production. It's all about Peter Pan meeting Alice in Wonderland and I want to be a Lost Boy. I thought if you rang your hairdresser,' said Jo, 'she might be able to fit me in right away. If you asked her as a special favour, I bet she could.'

There was a pause.

'Do you remember,' said Mrs Jameson, 'that in your first term at Peter's you were wild to let your hair *grow*, because you thought you wanted to be a ballet dancer? And then you decided that you didn't want to be a ballet dancer and so you had it all cut off again? And then do you remember all the scenes we had because you said it was hideous and ghastly and too short and you couldn't do anything with it? And so then you grew it again. And everybody said how nice it looked. And you were able to do things with it. And now you want to be a Lost Boy and have it all cut off again –'

'Yes, I do!' said Jo. 'I want it cut very, very short, like Tom's.'

'I suggest you get the part first and then we'll think about it.'

'But I won't get the part unless I look like a boy!'

'Oh, for goodness sake!' said Mrs Jameson. 'How many Lost Boys are there in Peter Pan?'

'*I* don't know!'

'Well, let's count them . . . Tootles, Nibs, Curly – Slightly, the Twins – that's half a dozen. Are you seriously telling me,' said Mrs Jameson, 'that there are half a dozen girls in your class who look like boys?'

'Yes! No! It's not just our class, it's everyone. And there are loads of people who have their hair really, really short. It's very fashionable,' said Jo. 'And just think how easy it would be to wash – I wouldn't keep using up all the shampoo and leaving bits in the wash-basin like you're always complaining about, and it would be *tidy*, not always getting in my eyes like it does now. It's very bad for you, having hair in your eyes. Plus I was told off today,' said Jo, 'for having it flopping all over the place.'

'That is entirely your own fault. I have no sympathy with you. You've got hair slides, you've got elastic bands – why not use them?'

'Because they break!' cried Jo. 'If my hair was short I wouldn't *need* hair slides and elastic bands . . . think how much money it'd save you!'

'Well, you can't have it cut this week, Lynn's on holiday. You'll have to wait till she gets back.'

'I can't wait! It's urgent! I don't mind if Lynn's not there, someone else can do it. Anyone can cut hair –'

'I'll make an appointment for Saturday week,' said Mrs Jameson. 'Let that satisfy you.'

'But I want it for Monday!' roared Jo. 'I want it for the audition! I want jam today, I don't w–'

'*Joanne!*' Her mother rounded on her sharply. 'All I ever seem to hear you say is *I want, I want, I want* . . . there are other people in this house, you know, besides yourself. The world does not centre on you, my girl, whatever you may think! I said Saturday week and I meant Saturday week. Any more of this selfish grizzling and you won't get it cut at all!'

Any normal parent would want to *help* their child, not *hinder* it. Jo banged up the stairs in a fury. Jam yesterday, jam tomorrow . . . why couldn't she have jam today, just for once? Other people did.

She looked at herself in the mirror. She didn't look in the *least* like a boy. Determinedly she marched along the passage to the bathroom and helped herself to the surgical scissors – long and sharp and pointy – from the bathroom cabinet. Then she went back to her bedroom and shut the door (hooking a chair under the handle just in case) and pulled out the stool from under her dressing table.

Jo's dressing table had a special sort of mirror, with a central panel and two wings, which meant that you could see the back of your head, which was exactly what you needed when you were trying to cut your own hair without leaving too many holes or making too many frilly bits. Even so, in spite of the special mirror, the hemline, as it were, was decidedly lopsided by the time she had finished, inclined either to slope steeply upwards to her left ear or fall sharply away to her right, depending which way you looked at it. There also, inexplicably, seemed to be a little bald spot in the middle, at the back, just *above* the hemline. She tried snipping away the hair on either side of the bald bit – styling it, she thought loftily – but that only made matters worse, so that the little bald bit was by now more of a large bald *patch*, which made it look as if she were suffering from mange. Never mind, she thought nervously; hair soon grew again. The front was what mattered. She flattered herself that the front looked rather good.

Her mother called up the stairs that her dad was in and tea was on the table. Boldly, carrying a pillowslip full of hair, Jo descended to the kitchen. Just at first, nobody noticed that she now looked like a boy (albeit a boy suffering from mange). She stalked past her dad to empty the pillowslip full of hair into the bin. Her dad glanced up as she passed.

'Good grief!' he said. 'What on earth have you done to yourself?'

Tom choked on his fish and chips and had to be walloped. Andy, walloping, said, 'What do you call that, then? The off-the-head look?' Mrs Jameson came over faint and had to sit down. She said, 'Jo, you are the end! Couldn't you even wait five minutes?'

'I told you,' said Jo, bursting into tears, 'I needed it for Monday!'

Afterwards, with Tom and Andy as interested spectators, Jo sat on a kitchen stool with a towel round her shoulders while first her dad ran his razor up the back of her neck and then her mum took the scissors to what was left. (Not very much.)

'It's kind of . . . spiky,' said Andy.

'Kind of bald,' said Tom.

'No, I like it,' said Andy. 'Makes her look elfin.'

'Elves aren't bald,' said Tom.

'She's not bald, she's got a tuft left on top and a few spokes over the forehead –'

'Like a sort of hedgehog, gone punk.'

'Like a pixie,' said Andy, 'with a crew cut.'

'I suppose it will grow,' said Mr Jameson.

The Gang, next day, were surprisingly (for the Gang) discreet about it.

'Nice and short,' said Fij.

'Trendy,' said Bozzy.

'At least it is different,' said Barge. 'That is the main thing.'

The main thing was what Sarah thought, but Sarah didn't say. Jo wasn't even sure that she noticed. They passed once in the Upper Corridor and once in the playground, but on both occasions Sarah was deep in discussion with Jasmine – talking about Lost Boys? – and hardly even glanced in Jo's direction. Michelle Wandres noticed, of course. She would. She said, 'I'm glad you got something done about that hair – but you didn't have to go to extremes!'

Jo thought – but couldn't be sure – that she was trying to be funny.

At the Club that evening, lurking by the door ready to attach himself to her, Robbie did a double take and said, 'You've had your hair cut!'

'He noticed,' said Matty.

Tom, who was a bit like Bozzy in some respects and didn't always recognize sarcasm when he heard it, gave a guffaw.

'Be hard not to . . . she looks like a hedgehog!'

'It is a bit short,' said Robbie, 'isn't it?'

Jo snapped, 'It was meant to be short – I *wanted* it short. I was sick of having it flopping about my face all the time.'

'It was nice, though,' said Robbie, 'when it was long.'

Jo tossed her head. (It still felt strange to toss her head and not feel hair flapping about.) 'I don't see why I should be expected to go round looking like a dish mop just because you like it!'

Robbie looked hurt. 'You didn't look like a dish mop!'

'Well, I felt like one.' It did *madden* her when Robbie put on that silly suffering expression.

'You needn't think,' said Matty, 'that the way we do our hair is done to keep you happy.'

'I don't!' said Robbie. He sounded like a sheep bleating, thought Jo.

'She wants to be a Lost Boy,' said Matty. 'Don't you?'

'She's a lesbian,' said Tom. 'They're all lesbians. All of 'em!'

Robbie looked startled.

'Leave 'em,' said Tom. 'Let 'em get on with it.'

'Yeah, we'd do a lot better without you lot!' screamed Matty, as Tom dragged a bewildered Robbie across the room.

'Who needs women anyway?' yelled Tom.

'Who needs men?' retorted Matty. 'Not us!'

Tom, without even bothering to turn round, stuck two fingers in the air. Matty shouted something unprintable.

'I can't stand boys,' she said.

Last term Jo had thought that she rather liked them; this term, she wasn't so sure. Perhaps they were all right when they were older, but at Tom's age they were either rebarbative, like Tom, or – well – *wet*. It had to be said. Always beaming and hanging about and making nuisances of themselves. Always ringing you up when you didn't want to be rung up, or hiding round corners and leaping out on you, all gooey and daft,

104

wanting to carry things, wanting to *do* things – see you over the road, help you onto the bus, as if you were a hundred and three and couldn't do it for yourself.

'Boys,' said Matty, 'are a pain.'

'They are,' said Jo. She ran her fingers through her spiky hair. 'They're a *pain*.'

9

The auditions were conducted by Jasmine and Sarah, jointly.

'Where are my Lost Boys?' cried Sarah. 'All my Lost Boys . . . over here with me!'

Jo was the first to scuttle across. She arrived, beaming, at Sarah's side, closely followed by Melanie and Lol (how did *Lol* think she could ever be a Lost Boy?) Katy Wells and Jan Hammond from Year 9 and a gaggle of teenies from Year 7. Nadge, grinning broadly, sauntered behind them.

'Playing Cards to me!' called Jasmine. The Playing Cards, being dancers, moved rather more elegantly across the Hall. 'March Hares? Any March Hares? March Hares over in the corner. Dormice? No Dormice? We must have *some* Dormice . . . all right, we'll leave the Dormice for the moment. It doesn't really matter, there aren't any lines. What about Mad Hatters? Any Mad Hatters?'

'Fancy no Dormice!' said Sarah. 'It's such a nice little part. . . . Jo, why aren't you up for it? You look like a natural, with your hair like that!'

Jo's bosom swelled indignantly. Who wanted to be a Dormouse, without any lines? She wanted to be one of Sarah's Lost Boys!

They were all divided up and given scripts with individual parts underlined in red. Jo was asked to read Slightly: so was Melanie. Melanie read well, as you would expect from someone whose uncle was in a TV soap, but there wasn't any sense in pretending that she looked like a boy because she didn't. She had a totally girlish sort of face, all pretty and delicate, and a girlish sort of voice, very light and rather fluting. She walked in a girlish sort of way, swaying her hips and taking tiny little mincing steps, and had girlish mannerisms such as flapping her hands and batting her eyelashes. She wasn't in the least athletic, as Jo was. She couldn't swarm up ropes in the Gym, right to the very top, or clamber about on the wall bars or do handstands on the horse. And anyway, what about her hair? You couldn't have a Lost Boy with long chestnut curls.

On the whole, Jo was quite hopeful. Nadge was obviously going to be chosen, simply because she *did* look like a boy, and even though she might not be too good at acting, she could do cartwheels and walk on her hands and swagger, which was what Sarah seemed to want. Well, Jo could do all those things, too. She was a member of the special gym team, wasn't she? She wondered, anxiously, if Sarah was aware of this. On her way out of the Hall at the end of the auditions, quite casually, as if it were a perfectly normal, everyday mode of locomotion, Jo upended herself and sidled crabwise through the doors on her hands. It was just unfortunate that Michelle should happen to be coming *in* through the doors at precisely the same moment. How was Jo supposed to know that Michelle would be

107

coming in? She wasn't a mind-reader, was she? And anyway, what was she coming in *for*? She wasn't anything to do with the auditions.

Michelle squawked as one of Jo's feet, clad in sturdy brown lace-ups (regulation wear for the lower orders) went *clonk*! into the side of her head. Jo promptly overbalanced and collapsed in a heap in front of Sarah, who had to put out a hand against the doorpost to steady herself.

'Joanne Jameson, it's you again!' Michelle's face, which was usually white and pinched, had gone all fat and purple. Her eyes squinted furiously in several directions behind her spectacles. 'What do you think you're doing with your bottom in the air, displaying your underwear to everyone?'

Giggles ran through the assembled ranks.

'If you think the spectacle of your knickers is an edifying one,' snarled Michelle, 'then you had better think again!'

Jo picked herself up, with what dignity she could muster.

'Next time,' murmured Sarah, as she moved past, 'you had better make sure you're wearing tights.'

It was so *humiliating*. But at least she had shown that she could walk on her hands just as well as Nadge.

Next morning when she went to look at the notice board, she found that she had been cast as the Dormouse.

'The *nerve* of it!' fumed Barge. The Gang felt it keenly. It was all very well having a named part, as opposed to simply being an assorted Playing Card and one of a pack, but what was the point of having a named part if all you did was sit with your head in a teapot?

'And in a beastly mouse costume!' wailed Jo.

'I expect you will have *some* lines,' said Fij.

'Well, I haven't! I looked at the script. It just says, *Dormouse snores* or *Dormouse whiffles* or *Mad Hatter picks up Dormouse's head and stuffs it in the teapot.*'

'And that is *all*?' said Fij, appalled.

'That is *all*,' wailed Jo.

'Well!'

The Gang looked at one another.

'If you ask me,' said Barge, stoutly, 'you'd be better out of it.'

'All you have to say is thank you very much but no thank you,' said Fij.

'Tell them,' urged Bozzy, 'that they cannot insult one of *us* with impinity.'

'Punity,' said Jo.

'It is punity,' said Bozzy. 'It's an absolutely *piffling* little part.'

'I suppose there is just a chance,' said Fij, 'that someone may fall under a bus.'

'Yes, like Melanie, for example. Then you could play her part, which is obviously what you ought to be playing.' Melanie had been cast in the role of Slightly. 'After all, you are at least as slight as she is, and *what*,' demanded Barge, 'is she intending to do with all that hair?'

Nobody knew what Melanie was intending to do with all her hair. When anyone asked her, she simply smiled an enigmatic smile and said, 'You'll have to wait and see, won't you?'

Since being given the part of Slightly, Melanie had become quite unbearable. Unlike Nadge, who was playing Curly with a modest and proper appreciation of her own limitations as an actress, Melanie flounced about as if she were Lady Macbeth and Desdemona rolled into one. She was glad, she said, that she hadn't been chosen to play Alice. Alice might have more words (she did: about ten times more) but Alice was *boring*. Anyone could play Alice. Slightly was a real challenge – which was why, of course, it had been given to her. Curly only had a couple of lines and spent most of the time clowning, and the Twins, played by two strange gnomelike beings from Year 7, only had to stand around sucking their thumbs, while Nibs and Tootles (Katy Wells and Jan Hammond) might *say* just as much as Slightly but it was Slightly who had all the really funny lines, such as for instance explaining why he was called Slightly, which wasn't because he was slight but because his mother had written it on the rompers that he was wearing when he got lost – 'Slightly Soiled: that's my name.'

It wasn't everyone, said Melanie, who could deliver a funny line and get a laugh. You had to have the technique: the technique was very important. Melanie had technique because of her uncle.

'It runs in the family. You either have it or you haven't. It's more of a feel than anything – knowing *how* to say a line and *when* to say a line. I suppose it's an instinct, really.'

'Instinct.' Lol and Ashley nodded, sagely.

'My uncle says that anyone can learn to move about the stage without knocking things over, but timing is a precious gift.'

'Precious gift –'

'That's what my uncle says.'

Melanie's uncle was coming to watch her (not to watch anyone else: just *her*). Melanie's uncle might bring his girlfriend with him. His girlfriend was a famous actress who was often on television, but she couldn't tell them who she was because it was a secret.

'Secret!' breathed Lol and Ash.

They would see her when she came, promised Melanie, and then they would know.

'You're bound to recognize her.'

'Recognize her!'

'My uncle says maybe, afterwards, you'll be able to get autographs.'

'Autographs!'

'It really,' said Barge, 'is just too sickmaking for words. And you see,' she said to Jo, 'what comes of trying to be helpful and do your bit and think of the House . . . you just get walked all over. Thrust aside for One who has Connections . . . I mean, who in their right minds would ever cast that flimmery flummery creature as a Boy?'

'Just because her uncle is some cruddy actor,' said Bozzy. 'That's all it is . . . just currying favour.'

Jo tried valiantly to pretend that it must have been Jasmine's doing – *Sarah* wouldn't try to curry favour – but she couldn't quite rid herself of the memory of

Sarah saying why didn't Jo try for the Dormouse – 'You look a natural, with your hair like that.' Sarah obviously hadn't even *considered* her for a Lost Boy.

'At least you do have a proper part, though,' said Fij, attempting solace as she and Jo walked up the road together after school. 'Everyone will see your name in the programme and know that the head in the teapot is yours. It could have been worse . . . you might not have got a part at *all*.'

Jo did her best to take comfort from this reflection. She looked again at her script, which Jasmine had handed out during the lunch break, and discovered that she did after all have a line – 'Twinkle, twinkle, twinkle, twinkle, twinkle, (etc.).' It wasn't, admittedly, much of a line (the stage direction said, *Dormouse shakes itself and begins singing in its sleep*) but with any luck she should be able to stretch it into half a dozen or so twinkles before the Mad Hatter or the March Hare burst in and dunked her again. It might get a laugh. And she could have fun with the whiffles and the squeaks. Perhaps it wasn't quite as bad as she had first thought. At least she would be on stage with Sarah and they would be at rehearsals together, and even if Jo *were* only whiffling and squeaking and saying twinkle, Sarah could hardly help but notice her.

The first rehearsal was on Thursday, after school. It was what Melanie called 'a read-through', which meant everyone sitting round the table in the Senior Library with their scripts. Sarah and her Boys – they were already being referred to as 'Sarah's Boys' – sat in a tight little huddle at one end, the tea party at the other.

(The Playing Cards hadn't been called.) There was much laughing and joking at Sarah's end of the table. All the Boys, except the two gnomes from Year 7, who were still a bit overawed, were being very forward and familiar, addressing Sarah as 'Pete' and saying things they wouldn't normally have dared to say. Melanie at one point even went so far as to suggest 'a bit of business . . . you know, on this line *here* where I say about the rompers . . . couldn't I pull out my handkerchief to show them, and the handkerchief could be a bit of old romper? The bit with *Slightly Soiled* written on it?'

Instead of squashing her flat, which was what, in Jo's opinion, she deserved, Sarah only laughed and said, 'Good idea! Did you hear that, Jas? Melanie's just come up with a really good bit of business.'

Nobody, least of all Sarah, took the slightest notice of Jo. There she was, crammed between a great gawking creature from Year 12 playing the Mad Hatter, and a pink plump pudding of a thing from Year 11 playing the March Hare, grunting and squeaking and whiffling whenever the script called for her to grunt or squeak or whiffle, and nobody even taking the trouble to acknowledge her. She might just as well not have been there, for all the impression she was making. Nobody said, 'Oh, great squeak, Jo!' or, 'Super grunt'. However, she did have her one line.

When you only had one line, you might as well make the most of it. Jo made the most of it.

'Twinkle twinkle twinkle, twinkle twinkle,' dirged

113

Jo, into her imaginary teapot. 'Twinkle twinkle twinkle, twinkle twinkle, twinkle, twinkle twinkle —'

She stopped, aware of an atmosphere. Everyone at the table had fallen silent and was looking at her.

'Twinkle, twinkle, twinkle, tw–'

'When you have quite finished,' said Jasmine.

' –inkle, twinkle —'

'Jo, do you have to be so childish?' said Sarah.

Cheeks burning, Jo said, 'I'm only saying what it says in the script . . . twinkle twinkle twinkle, twinkle twinkle.'

'You said it about two dozen times!' shrieked Melanie.

'Yes, because it says *etc*. Twinkle twinkle twinkle, twinkle twinkle – *etc*. That means it goes on,' said Jo.

Melanie groaned. Katy Wells and Jan Hammond exchanged delighted grins. Sarah shook her head, as if in disbelief.

Jasmine said, 'Caroline —' addressing the pink pudding girl playing the March Hare – 'at the third twinkle, could you and Yvonne' (Yvonne was the Mad Hatter) 'plunge the Dormouse back into its teapot and make sure that it stays there? You don't want to take things too literally, Jo. I don't mind the odd gurgle, but for heaven's sake preserve a sense of proportion!'

Jo hunched her shoulders up to her ears and slumped, batlike, on her chair. So! It had come to this . . . three twinkles and a gurgle. How could she be expected to shine by just saying twinkle twinkle twinkle *glup*? *No*body could. Not even – she sought for a name and failed to find one – not even the Queen. The Queen,

114

of course, wouldn't lower herself to say anything so stupid.

'Twinkle twinkle twinkle *glup*,' said the Queen, graciously. Brightly? *Magisterially*. 'Twinkle twinkle —'

'Jo?' said Jasmine. There was just a hint of impatience in her voice. 'Could we have your squeak here, please?'

'Do try to keep up,' urged Sarah. 'It's so unfair on the rest of the cast if one person just goes wandering off.'

'Squeak?' said Jasmine.

Jo squeaked, grumpily.

'The Dormouse is obviously sulking,' said Jasmine.

Everyone laughed except Sarah (and Jo).

At the end of the rehearsal Sarah came up to Jo and said, 'I hope you're not one of those people who can't take criticism, Jo. It's very important to remember that we are all part of a team.'

It was all very well *saying* that, but some parts of the team were obviously more highly regarded than other parts.

'Sarah said,' boasted Melanie, 'that she's going to invite all the Lost Boys round to her house for special rehearsals over half term. Sarah said that the Lost Boys are the most important part of the production. Sarah said that everything stands or falls by them. Sarah said —'

Sarah said, *Sarah said*. Jo's heart raged at some of the things that Sarah was supposed to have said.

The week before half term, Petersham Under-13s

played a home match against Fallowfield Under-13s and won handsomely by eighteen goals to nine. Jo scored ten of those eighteen goals: Sarah was nowhere to be seen.

'Absolutely *disgraceful*,' foamed Barge. 'House games captain and she doesn't even bother to watch when members of her own House are playing!'

Miss Duncan had watched, and Miss Duncan had said *well done*; but Miss Duncan wasn't Sarah. It turned out, afterwards, that Sarah had been coaching Slightly and the Twins in what Melanie grandly referred to as 'a rather complex piece of business . . . not complex for *me*, that is. But complex for the babies. She wanted me to give them the benefit of my experience.'

'Excuse me,' said Barge. 'Does anyone happen to have a plastic bag handy?'

'I've got a carrier,' said Bozzy. 'Why? What do you want it for?'

'I need it for being sick into,' said Barge. 'I have just come over very queer.'

'That's funny, so have I,' said Bozzy.

'Yes, me, too,' said Fij.

They passed the bag solemnly from one to another, ritually making vigorous vomiting noises into it.

'Jam?' Fij held it out to Jo. Jo shook her head. Melanie did make one feel sick, but she could cope with that. She was used to Melanie showing off. What she wasn't used to was being snubbed by Sarah. They had passed within *centimetres* in the corridor that morning, so close that they had practically touched, and

Sarah hadn't even bothered to look at her, let alone smile. There had to be something she could do.

Desperate times called for desperate measures.

'Help!' screeched Jo, falling flat at Sarah's feet at the bottom of the main staircase later in the day. She lay, artistically crumpled, one arm flung out, waiting for Sarah to come and pick her up.

Calmly, Sarah stepped over her.

'Jo, that is an extremely silly place to lie,' she said. 'I should get up if I were you, before you get trodden on.'

Jo groaned, sepulchrally.

'I shouldn't leave it too long.' Sarah's voice floated back to her. 'Michelle is not far behind.'

Jo moaned and stirred and slowly rolled over.

'Where am I?' she quavered. No one answered. Cautiously fluttering an eyelid, Jo saw to her indignation that Sarah had gone sailing on down the corridor for all the world as if there were no pathetic heap of body huddled at the foot of the stairs.

'Help!' whimpered Jo. She scrambled to her feet and went reeling after Sarah, down the corridor. 'I fainted!' said Jo.

'Oh, really?' said Sarah. 'You could have fooled me. I thought you were practising stage falls.'

It seemed safer, on the whole, to ignore this heartless remark. (Sarah surely couldn't *mean* it?)

'One minute I was standing there,' said Jo, 'and the next minute —' she put a hand to her head and staggered drunkenly against the wall – 'the next minute everything went all funny and fuzzy and – and the floor came up to meet me. I must have passed out,' said Jo.

'It's the first time I've ever seen anyone pass out by leaping six feet in the air in a vertical take-off.' Sarah said it crushingly. 'This is the main corridor, you know, not the playground.'

Sarah swept on her way. Jo, rubbing her knee where she had banged it in her rapid descent floorwards, trailed after her.

'What happened?' Bozzy suddenly appeared, panting and pop-eyed, at her elbow. 'I was up there —' she gestured vaguely towards the ceiling – 'when I saw you suddenly go *whoosh*! And then I saw you sort of – sort of *arranging* yourself on the ground.'

'I was not *arranging* myself,' said Jo. 'I *fainted*.'

'Oh! Is that what you were doing? I thought you were dancing,' said Bozzy. She thought about it for a moment. 'What were you doing it for? Any particular reason?'

Honestly! There were times when Bozzy was so thick. Did she think people fainted on purpose?

'I suppose Sarah came and picked you up?' said Bozzy.

'No.' Jo said, bitterly. 'She *stepped* over me.'

'You're lucky she didn't step *on* you,' said Bozzy. She sniggered, well pleased with her own wit.

Some people, thought Jo, were so supportive.

'Neil desperado!' said Bozzy. 'You never know . . . p'raps Melanie will go down with the galloping pox.'

10

Jo couldn't wait for Melanie to go down with the pox, galloping or otherwise. Already it was half term, and what had she done to impress Sarah? Nothing! She had started off so well, being seen with her new netball and being congratulated and encouraged and told that 'that was the stuff'. What had happened to make it all go wrong?

What had happened was that Sarah had suddenly lost all interest in netball – well, no, that wasn't quite true. She hadn't lost *all* interest, she still played for the House and helped coach the House teams, but she certainly wasn't as keen as she had been. This horrible Peter Pan and Alice thing had taken over. It was – apparently – supposed to be funny. Jo herself couldn't see what the joke was, though Jasmine and Sarah, and any other prefects who wandered into rehearsals, screeched with laughter. So did Melanie, who almost certainly couldn't see the joke any more than Jo but liked to pretend that she could. Every time Sarah laughed, Melanie laughed too. She and Sarah had become thick as thieves. Sarah kept saying things like, 'Come on, Melanie! You're the pro. Give me some ideas!' or 'What do you think, Melanie? What would your uncle say?'

Melanie had told her – Melanie had told *everyone* – that her uncle was coming to watch the performance. She had promised Sarah that she would introduce her. Sarah, it seemed, had ambitions to go on the stage. She was hoping that Melanie's uncle would be able to give her some advice. Even if Jo *had* been playing a Lost Boy instead of a mouldy Dormouse, she could never have competed with that.

She lay glumly in bed on the first day of the holiday, twitching her toes under the duvet and wishing she were Melanie. On Monday afternoon, Melanie and 'the Boys' were all going round to Sarah's for their special rehearsal. Jo didn't even know where Sarah lived.

On sudden impulse, she threw back the duvet and went padding downstairs in her pyjamas to the telephone table in the hall. Sitting cross-legged on the hall floor with the local directory in her lap, she ran her finger down the list of Biggs. There weren't very many of them. Bigg, E.; Bigg, John; Bigg, R.J.C.; Bigg, Dr T. – that must be the one! She remembered Lol fulsomely talking about Sarah's dad as Dr Bigg – 'Dr Bigg's one of our best customers, Dr Bigg's a wonderful man. Dr Bigg is *brilliant*.'

She looked at the address: 14 Hillview Crest, Meadowlands. Meadowlands was where Robbie lived; it wasn't too far away. She could easily get there on her bike. Of course, she wouldn't go *bothering* Sarah. She wouldn't knock on the door or anything like that; that would be presumptuous. All she wanted was just to

120

look, to see the place where Sarah lived. If she was very lucky, she might even see Sarah herself.

Jo put the telephone book away and stood up.

'What's this?' cried Mr Jameson, coming out of the kitchen with early-morning cups of tea for him and Jo's mum. 'What's got you out of bed before midday?'

'I have things to do,' said Jo.

'Well, I hope they don't include telephoning . . . my telephone bill can't stand much more of you and your brothers.'

'I am not going to telephone,' said Jo. 'I am going to go somewhere.

First thing after breakfast she was on her bike, pedalling furiously through the side roads to Meadowlands. Meadowlands was what her mum called 'the posh part' of Petersham. Andy said it was where the nobs lived, although Robbie lived there and he wasn't a nob, at least she didn't think he was, but Robbie only lived on the outskirts, in a perfectly ordinary house a bit like the houses that Jo and Matty lived in. Sarah lived right up at the top, on the ridge, looking out over Petersham Common and St Mary's Hill, in a great sprawling old-fashioned house with chimneypots and ivy and criss-cross windows and an all-round garden properly fenced off both back and front and a front gate which said *No hawkers No Circulars*. Jo had *always* wanted to live in a house like that. She had once asked her mother why they couldn't, and the answer had come back, 'Because we're not made of money.' Sarah's parents obviously were.

All the houses in Sarah's road were large and sprawling, with their own private front gardens. Slowly, with the air of one who was merely out for a Saturday-morning spin, Jo freewheeled on her bicycle past Aberlour and Little Garth and Burnt Pines down to the small grass roundabout at the bottom and back up again, pedalling hard and bright beetroot because of the hill, past The Willows and The Hollies and Ivy Mount, until she reached Sarah's, which was called Ridgehanger – because, she supposed, it hung right over the ridge.

Three times she cycled up and down Hillview Crest, but there were no signs of life at all coming from Ridgehanger. Not wanting to be in any way conspicuous, because after all one didn't normally go up and down the same stretch of road for hours on end if one was simply out for a spin, Jo set off round the block: down Foxearth Road, which went on for ever, up Three Oaks Rise, which was so steep she had to get off halfway and walk, along Kingscote Lane and back into familiar territory. Aberlour, Little Garth, Burnt Pines . . .

By eleven o'clock, when she had been doing her circuit for nearly two hours, she knew them all off by heart. Her legs were aching from so much pedalling uphill, and she hadn't seen a single solitary soul go either in or out of Ridgehanger. On one of her circuits she passed Robbie going in the opposite direction, on foot. They stopped to talk, Robbie all pink and apologetic because he assumed automatically that Jo was on her way to see him whereas he was on his way to see Tom.

122

'I'm not on my way anywhere,' said Jo. 'I'm just cycling about.'

'I'd go back and get my bike and cycle about with you,' said Robbie, 'if I hadn't promised to meet Tom . . . I said I'd meet him outside school.'

'You'd better go, then, hadn't you?' said Jo, eager to get back on her circuit. (Sarah could be coming out of Ridgehanger right this very moment.)

'I wouldn't have said I'd meet him if I'd known you were going to be here,' said Robbie.

'You'd better not keep him waiting,' said Jo. 'He'll only get in one of his sulks.'

'Yes. Well. I s'ppose –' Robbie broke off, awkwardly. Then his face suddenly brightened. 'I'm coming to see your end-of-term show!'

'I can't imagine why,' said Jo. 'I'm only playing a Dormouse.'

'We've got to,' said Robbie. 'We've said we'll buy tickets.'

'Oh?' Jo, immediately and perversely, felt slighted: so he wasn't coming to see *her*. 'Who from?'

'This person my mother knows who knows somebody who goes to your school and has got something to do with it.'

'Sarah?'

Robbie looked blank.

'Sarah Bigg? Or Jasmine Patel?'

'I don't know her name,' said Robbie.

Useless! Utterly useless!

'Well, don't come on my account,' said Jo.

'I'm not, it's this woman,' said Robbie. 'She's always

making my mother buy things she doesn't want. But of course I am looking forward to seeing *you*.'

Idiot! thought Jo, as she pounded back up Three Oaks Rise.

On Sunday morning, Jo woke up and had this really brilliant idea. She went next door to call on Matty.

'You know this competition you were going in for? This one where you had to take pictures of people and their pets? Did you ever get any pictures of pets?'

'I got Jool's brother's guinea pig,' said Matty. 'And one of next door's rabbit.'

'That doesn't sound very interesting.'

'No, well, I told you . . . I don't know many people with pets.'

'If we went over the Common,' said Jo, 'we might bump into Bozzy going for her Sunday-morning ride. You could take a picture of her and her horse.'

She knew that Bozzy went for rides on Sunday mornings because Bozzy had told them, not once but several times and in great detail. She rode a pony called Cobbles, whom she would have taken home and taken to bed with her if her parents hadn't put their feet down. They knew every ditch, every stream, every tussock of grass that Cobbles had ever jumped, every overhanging branch he had ever distinguished himself by avoiding, every rabbit that had made him shy – 'Poor darling! It wasn't his fault' – every other horse that had it in for him – 'Tried to *kick* him, on his poor little fetlock!'

'A horse would count as a pet, wouldn't it?' said Jo. 'You might even get a picture of Bozzy falling off.'

'Yeah, that would be fun,' said Matty.

'So shall we go?'

'What, right now?'

'Eleven o'clock.'

Eleven o'clock was when they set out from the stables. It took them, according to Bozzy, five minutes to reach Petersham Woods and another ten minutes to get through the Woods and on to the Common – and Sarah was always, *always* with them. Sarah never missed a ride, Bozzy said. She went riding twice every weekend – 'even if it's pouring'.

It wasn't pouring this morning, which was just as well as Matty might not have been able to take pictures in the rain, and if she couldn't have taken pictures, she wouldn't have come, and Jo wasn't sure that she was brave enough to go by herself. It would have looked – well – *obvious*, to be hanging about over the Common all by herself. She wouldn't want Sarah to think she was spying on her.

By quarter past eleven, Jo and Matty were in position, standing under the horse-ride sign – *Horse Ride: No Galloping* – at the side of the bridle path where it came out of the woods.

'They should be here in a minute,' said Jo.

Matty, who wore her camera slung round her neck like a real photographer, raised it to her eyes and squinted through it, efficiently twiddling at various knobs and dials as she did so. Getting the focus, Jo supposed. Jo wasn't into photography. She had tried, because of keeping up with Matty, but all her photographs came out either blurred or lopsided, or sometimes both together. Sometimes they didn't come out at all. Even when they did you couldn't always recognize what they were photographs of, like the ones she had taken of Tom's left ear and the back of her dad's head.

'I think I can hear something,' said Matty.

Jo could hear something, too. It sounded like a cavalry charge crunching and thundering through the trees.

'They must be running,' said Matty.

'I don't think you call it r–'

The words died on Jo's lips. With a great roaring and stamping a huge chestnut horse had come crashing out of the woods. Nostrils flared and hoofs pounding, it charged towards them down the bridle path. Sitting on top of it, a small frightened figure clinging to the reins, was Sarah . . .

For once in her life, Jo didn't hesitate. Fearlessly, she dashed forward, waving her arms, into the path of the oncoming horse.

Matty screamed. Someone else shouted. Clammy hands gripped Jo's insides. The horse was right on top of her . . .

Horses, on the whole, have no wish to mow people down. They mostly prefer to go round obstacles rather than over them, though a few, left to themselves, will simply crash straight through. Sarah's, fortunately, was one of the more considerate. At the sight of a frenzied figure dancing, doll-like, in its path, it did a spectacular leap sideways, kicked up its heels and galloped on. Not so fortunately, having done an equally spectacular leap in the opposite direction, its rider remained behind.

Jo stood transfixed, watching in a kind of horrified fascination as Sarah flew in a slow half-circle through the air, landing with a bump, upside down, on her riding hat. At the same time, out of the woods, *trit-trot*, *trit-trot*, bouncing up and down like a row of little corks, came all the rest of the ride. Jo had just time to catch a glimpse of Bozzy, pop-eyed with astonishment, all round and dumpy in her anorak and riding breeches, when a shout came from the back of the column, 'Stop that horse!' and instantly half a dozen little corks, including Bozzy, went cantering joyously off along the bridle path, within centimetres of Jo and Matty, in pursuit of the galloping chestnut. Sarah, already, was on her feet and dusting herself down. She strode up to Jo, her face scarlet and contorted.

'Well, thank you *very* much! That was just what I needed . . . some idiot leaping out in front of me!'

A terribly shaky feeling had crept up Jo's legs and somehow got into her stomach. She felt cold and trembly and sick.

'I thought you were being run away with,' she whispered.

'You thought *what*?'

Before Jo had a chance to repeat it, a lean, hatchet-faced woman wearing a bowler hat, with her hair in a pink hair net, had come barking up from the rear of the column on a big black horse the size of an elephant.

'OK, Sarah? No bones broken? Just as well, entirely

your own fault – and another time, *keep hold of those reins*! Horse running about loose all over the place . . . lucky for you they've managed to catch it. Your dad would have had my guts for garters, the money he paid for that nag. As for you, child –' Jo shrivelled – 'you do know this is a bridle path, I suppose? You do know what that means? It means that horses have priority. You wouldn't go running across a main road without looking, would you? Well, then! Don't go running across bridle paths without looking. You could have caused a nasty accident. *Don't do it again.* All right?'

Jo nodded, not trusting herself to speak.

'Right! The ignorance of some of you townies has to be seen to be believed.'

Hatchet Face turned, abruptly, and went trotting off, up-down, up-down, stiff as a ramrod, to rejoin the rest of the column, all bunched together at the far end of the path with the recaptured horse.

'I begin to think,' hissed Sarah, venomously, at Jo, as she took off after Hatchet Face, 'that you must be half-witted!'

Jo and Matty walked home in silence. Matty, perhaps, was being tactful; Jo still felt too shaky to speak.

'I'll tell you what,' said Matty, as they turned into their road. 'I got a smashing photo of Sarah. I'm going to call it "Parting Company" . . . that was really brilliant, you running out like that. It was almost like you did it on purpose, just so I could get a good shot. I know you *didn't*,' said Matty, 'but that's what it looked like.'

If it had looked like that to Matty, what must it have looked like to Sarah?

'If you like,' said Matty, 'I'll give you half my prize money, if I win. After all,' she said, generously, 'I couldn't have done it without you.'

11

Needless to say, Bozzy had lost no time in bustling round to see Barge and give her the news of Jo's latest exploit. Jo found herself accosted the minute she walked into school on their first day back after half term.

'Whatever,' screeched Bozzy, 'did you think that you were doing?'

'What *was* she doing?' Fij, who hadn't heard, craned eagerly across.

'Well, that is what we should like to know,' said Barge. 'Running out in front of people's horses!'

'Running out in front of *Sarah's* horse,' said Bozzy.

'*Sarah's* horse?' Fij looked at Jo, big-eyed.

'She was absolutely furious,' said Bozzy, 'specially as Miss Rafferty told her off.'

'Told Sarah off?'

'For galloping,' said Bozzy. 'You're not supposed to gallop over the Common. But then you're not supposed,' she added, 'to rush about on bridle paths.'

'She could have been *killed*,' said Fij.

'Sarah could have been killed,' said Bozzy.

'And you still haven't told us,' said Barge, 'what you did it for.'

Jo adopted the loftiest tone of which she was capable. 'I had my reasons,' she said.

'Well, yes, I dare say you did. Nobody does things without a reason. Not unless they are totally mindless, which on the whole you are not, though having this thing about Sarah has certainly *reduced* you somewhat. What we want to know, however,' said Barge, 'is what those reasons were.'

'Of course, you don't have to tell us if you don't want,' said Fij, 'but it would be a comfort to know that you haven't actually gone *stark* staring bonkers.'

'You weren't trying to do away with yourself, I suppose?' Barge asked the question carelessly. 'Girl-throws-herself-under-horse sort of thing?'

'Frustrated teenager Joanne Jameson –'

'Why frustrated?' said Bozzy.

'Because of having been Overlooked in Favour of Another,' said Barge. She nodded at Fij. 'Continue.'

'Frustrated teenager, Joanne Jameson,' said Fij, reading from an imaginary paper, 'finding herself typecast as a teapot-incarcerated Dormouse in her House end-of-term production, yesterday hurled herself under the hoofs of an oncoming horse in a desperate bid to draw attention to her plight. . . . Said Joanne yesterday, "It is not that I have anything against Dormice but it is difficult to distinguish oneself with one's head stuffed in a teapot. And to add insult to injury," she added, "I am not a tea drinker." The horse in question belonged to the lovely and delectable Sarah B–'

'Jo!'

Jo jumped; so did Fij.

131

'If I might have a quick word?' said Sarah.

This was it; now even the part of the Dormouse was going to be taken off her.

'I still haven't the faintest idea,' said Sarah, scarcely bothering to move out of range of the quivering antennae of Barge & Co., 'what you thought you were up to the other day, but I feel I should accept some part of the blame for what occurred. I should not, of course, have been galloping in the first place. For that, I apologize. Having said that, however. . . . ' Sarah paused. 'One does not expect idiots to come jumping out at one in the middle of a bridle path!'

'I am most terribly sorry,' mumbled Jo.

'Well, I should hope you are! It was absolutely cretinous. As a matter of interest, did you really think I was being run away with?'

Jo nodded, unhappily.

'Well, for goodness' sake!' said Sarah.

Naturally the Gang had heard; how could they not? Standing there with their great elephantine ears flapping. Bozzy marvelled, and continued to do so, scornfully and at frequent intervals throughout the day.

'Fancy not being able to tell when a person is in control and when a person is being run away with!'

'You'd think *any*one would know when a horse was bolting.'

'She was just giving him his head . . . I mean, it was so *obvious*.'

Jo could see, looking back, that it probably was – or should have been. Bozzy wasn't to know of her secret daydreams. When you had nightly performed heroic

132

acts of rescue in the safety of your bed, tucked cosily away beneath the duvet, it was difficult not to leap to the wrong conclusion when the opportunity finally seemed to present itself.

'You'd hardly have to be an expert,' said Bozzy, '*I* wouldn't have thought.'

It was Barge, of all people, who leapt to Jo's defence.

'What you and your tiny mind would or would not think is totally irrelevant. People who are under the impression,' said Barge, witheringly, 'that Madras is the capital of Spain –'

'That was a mistake!'

'So was what Jammy did. It just so happens that yours proceeded from total ignorance, whereas she at least had Good Intentions. If you ask me,' said Barge, 'she deserves a medal.'

'Hear, hear!' said Fij.

'And if you *also* ask me, Miss High-and-Mighty Bigg is not worthy of being worshipped from afar. Here is Jam, offering her her all, *hurling* herself to the rescue –'

'She didn't need to be rescued!' screeched Bozzy.

'That is beside the point, you dumb twit. The point is that Jam *thought* she did. And if she *had've* done, then Jam would most likely have saved her life, and if you want my opinion,' said Barge, who was in the habit of giving her opinion whether people wanted it or not, 'if you want to know what *I* think, I think that a person that isn't grateful when another person saves their life doesn't deserve to have their life saved. It seems to me,' said Barge, 'that since going to America Sarah

133

has got rather too big-headed for her boots.' There was a pause. 'Or her hat,' added Barge, 'as the case may be.'

'She doesn't wear a –' began Bozzy, predictable as ever. She stopped. 'Well, she wears a *riding* hat. It was probably the only thing,' said Bozzy, ghoulishly, 'that stopped her being killed.'

A shiver ran through Jo. She wished they wouldn't keep talking about it. Even Barge, trying to be helpful, was only making matters worse. How could you expect a person to be grateful to someone who had idiotically rushed out in front of them and got them thrown off their horse? Sarah could have broken her neck – and it would all have been Jo's fault.

'What she *ought* to do,' said Fij, 'is make Melanie play the Dormouse and give Melanie's part to Jam . . . as a sort of reward, you know. Like the MBE. For services rendered.'

Reward? thought Jo, feeling slightly hysterical. For nearly breaking someone's neck?

'You never know,' said Barge. 'Stranger things have happened.'

'Not that strange,' muttered Jo.

'Look on the bright side,' said Bozzy. 'Think of Neil.'

'Who's Neil?'

'Neil Desperado!' cackled Bozzy.

There were times when Bozzy was a complete ninny.

The second half of term was just about as hateful as could be. They had hardly been back more than a week when an interhouse meeting was called, for Seventh and Eighth Years, in the Main Hall. They were to be talked at, according to Bozzy, who tended to be a scavenger where odd bits of information were concerned, by Miss Chidzey, the Deputy Head. Nobody liked Miss Chidzey; she was mean and crabby at the best of times. Today she was even meaner and crabbier than usual.

It had come to her notice, she said, pinching her nostrils tightly together as if the assembled pupils sitting cross-legged before her on the Hall floor were some kind of garbage heap giving off obnoxious odours, that Certain Members of the Lower School had spent the first half of term deliberately making a nuisance of themselves with some of the seniors.

'Their behaviour –' the nostrils flared: the Chiseller drew a deep, disdainful sniff up the length of her nose – 'has been more what I should expect of Goths and guttersnipes than young ladies of this establishment.'

A slight bristling ran through the ranks of the Eighth Years: who ever said they were supposed to be ladies? The Seventh Years shuffled their bottoms on the floor and looked nervous. Jo kept her head bent, staring down at her hands in her lap. It was a moment when she most fervently wished she had not sliced off her hair; it would have been a comfort, now, to have it hanging round her face.

The Chiseller, in her horrid crackly voice, went on to enumerate the various ways in which these 'ill-mannered female louts', as she called them, had sought to draw attention to themselves. They included running and shrieking in the corridors (Jo glanced quickly side-

135

ways at Barge, but Barge had her head tilted back and seemed to be inspecting something of great interest on the ceiling), lurking in bunches at the school gates (at least she had never done *that*), jostling and pushing at one another 'in what I can only call a most unseemly fashion', going out of their way to render themselves obvious (Jo's cheeks lit up like twin beacons) and generally, concluded the Chiseller, *pestering*. She didn't specify what manner of pestering but warned them, 'if there should be any repetition – if this immature and uncouth behaviour does not cease *forthwith* – then those guilty of it will find themselves in trouble. I shall not at this stage spell out who they are; they will know well enough. Go back now to your classes, and reflect upon what I have said.'

Jo slunk out of the Hall with her head hunched down between her shoulders.

'Such a relief,' said Fij, at break, 'to know that she can't possibly have been referring to us.'

'Well! I should hope not indeed.' Barge swaggered, indignantly. '*I* certainly do not recall lurking in any bunches, *or* going out of my way to render myself obvious. If I *am* obvious,' said Barge, 'then that is just the way I am. Some of us are, some of us aren't. It's a question of personality.'

'I suppose we may have shrieked a bit in corridors,' said Bozzy. 'And there was that time Jam dived head-first down the stairs.'

'Yes, but not on *purpose*,' said Fij.

'Well, no, but Sarah might have thought so.'

Jo turned pale.

'Look, it isn't anything to *do* with Sarah. Honestly,' said Fij. 'Debra Wilson told me. There's this group of Seventh Years who've gone potty over Philippa Sacks –'

'Philippa *Sacks*?'

Philippa Sacks was head of York. She really didn't have anything going for her, as far as Jo could see. Not like Sarah.

'Debra said they keep hanging about outside the Prefects' Room and trailing her along the corridors and – well, *lurking in bunches*,' said Fij.

'And pestering,' said Barge. 'I wonder how they pester?'

'Oh! I don't know . . . interrupting conversations and popping up all over the place and just sort of . . . *looming*, I suppose. But anyway,' said Fij, comfortably, 'it isn't anything to do with us.'

Jo wished she could be sure. How terrible it would be if Sarah had complained! She never smiled at Jo these days, when they passed in the corridor. Jo could have been just anybody. She never even spoke to her at rehearsals. Jo thought sadly that it was perfectly understandable. She thought most people probably wouldn't feel like talking to someone who had nearly killed them.

One day at rehearsal Jasmine announced that she and Sarah had been thinking. What they had been thinking was that as the Lost Boys were a very important part of the play without actually having tremendous numbers of lines to say, it would be a good idea if other people who also didn't have tremendous numbers of lines to say (but weren't such an important part of the play) should act as understudies – 'Just in case. It seems a wise precaution. What with flu epidemics and the like.'

The only people who could safely be dispensed with in an emergency were Playing Cards – and the Dormouse.

'Of course we'd have to *have* a Dormouse, but it's the sort of part anyone could pick up at almost a moment's notice. Would you mind awfully, Jo, if we asked you to learn Slightly?'

It was all Jo needed. (She could almost *hear* Melanie preening herself.)

'I'm sorry to lumber you with it.' Jasmine smiled; sweetly and apologetically. 'I know it's not what you volunteered for, but Melanie *has* offered to understudy Alice, which isn't something we would ever have asked of her.'

So why had she volunteered, stupid cow? Just to make an impression, no doubt. Or perhaps she had been secretly yearning to play the part of Alice all along, in spite of what she had said earlier about it being so boring. She was probably hoping that Tasmin might fall down a sewer and disappear.

'Is that all right, Jo? Can we rely on you?'

Jo looked across the room to where Sarah sat with the other Lost Boys, but Sarah was laughing at something the Twins had said – even *they* were familiar with her, now – and didn't even glance in Jo's direction. Jo said sullenly, 'Yes, I suppose so.' She wished she had the strength of mind to say no, but she wasn't quite brave enough for that.

'Understudies *are* important,' said Jasmine, 'and we did want to have at least one actress amongst them. After all, the Playing Cards are only dancers, really.'

It was what Jo's mum called 'soft soap'. But they're not soft-soaping *me*, thought Jo. It was bad enough being asked to understudy at all; but to be asked to understudy *Melanie* – that, thought Jo, was the end.

Jo flounced back to seek solace with the Gang. They were as outraged as she could have wished them to be.

'The nerve of it!'

'*You* understudy *her*?'

'The part should have been yours anyway!'

'She *still* hasn't done anything about her hair.'

Whenever anyone asked Melanie about her hair she just smiled, secretively and in an irritatingly superior fashion, and said, 'Not telling you.'

Now that Jo was officially her understudy, she became quite unbearably puffed up and patronizing and kept offering Jo the benefit of her totally unwanted advice.

'That business I do with the handkerchief when I make my first entrance . . . I shouldn't try *that*, if I were you. It can be a bit tricky.'

'So long as you get the lines off and know where to stand, that's the main thing. No one expects too much of an understudy.'

'Whatever you do, for heaven's sake don't try changing the interpretation. Just do it the way I do it – well,' simpered Melanie, 'as best you can.'

'Hope she falls down a sewer,' muttered Jo.

'We could always arrange it,' said Bozzy.

'Yes, well, if you do, make sure it's really grotty and yucky and *stinky*.'

Netball seemed to be the only aspect of Jo's life which was working out satisfactorily. She played in another three matches for the School Under-13s, scoring more than nineteen goals and having her name read out in Morning Assembly. She peered through her eyelashes to check that Sarah was listening, only to find that Sarah wasn't there. Neither, when she looked further, were Melanie or Nadge. It turned out they had all been given permission to miss Assembly for a Special Lost Boys run-through. Jo's heart swelled and very nearly burst with the injustice of it.

'Sarah is just so-o-o-o wonderful,' crooned Melanie. 'For someone who has no theatrical connections, she is going about things in a most professional way. I have helped her, of course. But the main thing is, she is capable of *learning*. Lots of amateurs aren't. I am going to ask my uncle,' she confided, ostensibly to a gape-eyed Lol and Ashley, but in fact to the entire room, 'to invite her out to supper with us after the show. I think it is the least one can do.'

'Help!' cried Barge. 'Gimme a plastic bag, someone, quick!'

The bag was produced; the sounds of ritual retching were heard. This time, Jo joined in.

'Naturally,' said Melanie, linking her arms through those of her faithful hench people, 'you two will be introduced as well, and will be able to shake his hand.'

140

'His hand!' moaned Barge.

Bozzy screamed. Fij shouted, 'Watch out, everyone, here I come!' and pitched herself floor-wards, full-length in the gangway.

'Felicity Jarvis,' said Mrs Stanley, arriving for her Maths class, 'what are you doing lying on the floor?'

'She fainted,' said the Mouse.

'It was too much for her,' said Emma.

'What was? What are you talking about?'

'The hand!' wailed the Bookends, in unison.

'I hope you haven't been watching video nasties,' said Mrs Stanley. 'Felicity, get up this instant – and take your head out of that plastic bag, Margery! Has no one ever told you it's dangerous? Really, I don't know what the matter is with you people today!'

'We are all feeling rather nauseous,' said Barge.

'Are you indeed? How very unfortunate, when you have a Maths class to face! Never mind! A good brisk trot round a few circumferences will soon put you to rights. Now, homework, please! Melanie, would you do the honours?'

With her superior smile just faintly lingering on her lips, Melanie oozed out of her desk and sallied sinuously up the gangway, one hand on her hip, the other languidly held out, palm upwards, to receive the night's offerings. Jo, slapping her Maths book on top of the pile, gritted her teeth and thought of sewers . . . grotty and yucky and *stinky*.

One Friday, Nellie's Under-14s had an after-school match against York, which meant Jo being late for rehearsal.

'Will it be all right?' said Jo. She consulted Jasmine, for Jasmine was, after all, the producer. It wasn't really anything to do with Sarah. Sarah might have helped write the show, and she might be playing one of the leads, but she wasn't the one who was responsible for actually putting it on. 'Is it OK if I turn up a bit late?'

'Well. . . . ' Jasmine hesitated. 'We'd better consult Sarah. She's House games. Sal!'

She turned and yelled across the Prefects' Room. Jo's ears boggled. So they did call her Sal!

'Jo says you've put her down for a match after school tomorrow. That means she'll miss the first part of the rehearsal. What do you want her to do? Play or rehearse?'

'Oh, she can play.' Unlike Jasmine, Sarah had no hesitation. 'The Dormouse isn't that important, it's only a few squeaks.'

It wasn't until later, when she had recovered from the first shock of hearing Sarah actually *say*, out loud, what she had long suspected – that the Dormouse was only a few mouldy unimportant squeaks – that Jo realized: *Jasmine* was the producer, but *Sarah* had made the decision. She began to wonder if perhaps Sarah was just a little bit bossy.

The Under-14s won their match against York by the comfortable margin of fourteen goals to eight, which meant they only had to beat Sutton to come top of the Junior League. Jo went bouncing jubilantly off to her rehearsal to report the good news.

'We won!' she hissed at Sarah. 'By f–'

'Not now, Jo!' Sarah flapped an irritable hand. 'For goodness' sake! We're trying to rehearse.'

Crestfallen, Jo turned away – but not before she had seen Melanie rolling her eyes to heaven. Grotty, yucky and *stinky*.

At the end of the rehearsal, Jasmine announced that the following Thursday, in the lunch hour, she was calling an understudy rehearsal – 'So will all understudies please make sure they know their lines.' She looked at Jo as she said it, Jo being the only understudy then present.

'I hope you will know your lines, Jo,' said Sarah, as they left the Hall. 'There's no point in being an understudy if you don't. What was it you were trying to say to me, by the way?'

Jo brightened. 'We won the match – against York. Fourteen to eight.'

'Good,' said Sarah. 'So you ought. York are quite useless.'

On the whole, Jo was a fairly conscientious person. She might occasionally skimp on her homework, or even, in a crisis, copy from Fij, but homework was fair game. If she was asked to do something personally, or as part of a team, when people were relying on her, she did it to the best of her ability. She struggled, therefore, to learn her lines for Thursday's understudy rehearsal, though it was difficult to rouse much enthusiasm for the task. She did it slowly and resentfully, begrudging every moment, only to find, when the day came, that none of the others had more than a mere passing acquaintance with what they were supposed to be saying.

'I told them,' said Claire. 'I said I hadn't got the time.'

Claire, who was one of the Playing Cards, had ballet classes every night, so in her case it was probably true and she genuinely didn't have time. The others simply hadn't bothered. Jo wished that she hadn't, either. She had spent *ages* sitting on her own in the kitchen, when she could have been in with the rest of the family watching television. And all for what? Melanie obviously wasn't going to fall down any sewers, and Tamsin Marshall, playing Alice, was looking almost indecently healthy, so there wasn't the remotest chance of Jo ever being asked to go on. It wasn't even as if Sarah were there to note the fact that Jo at least had taken the trouble to learn her lines. The rehearsal was being conducted by Jasmine on her own. The only person who had come to watch was Melanie, who sat on top of the box (they were rehearsing in the Gym) nonchalantly swinging her legs and eating buns and every now and again covering her face or rolling her eyes or audibly groaning.

The understudy rehearsal was, quite frankly, a disaster. Everyone except Jo had to read from a script: no one except Jo took it seriously. It was far more fun to fool around and speak in silly squeaky 'little boy' voices, and kick at each other and start pretend fights, than to get on with the business of rehearsing for parts they were never going to play. In the end Jo became infected as well and started fooling around with the rest of them, exaggerating all her moves, walking about bow-legged, like a cowboy without his horse, saying all her lines in a mock American accent just for the fun of it. Jasmine, attempting to read the part of Peter as well as keep control, was fighting a losing battle and knew it. For a brief moment, when Melanie jumped up to be Alice for them, order was restored – Melanie had a strange kind of authority once she was on stage – but then Claire stared hopping on one foot, and someone else decided to crawl, Jo collapsed into giggles and everything promptly fell to pieces.

'Honestly,' said Melanie. 'So *unprofessional*.'

'I couldn't agree more!' A voice called down from the gallery, which ran round three sides of the Gym. 'I've never seen such a disgraceful exhibition . . . I hope you're all thoroughly ashamed of yourselves!'

It was Sarah. She had been there all the time . . .

12

'. . . just absolutely *the* worst thing I have ever seen. Sarah was positively *foaming*.'

'Foaming!' breathed Ashley.

'Foaming,' nodded Lol.

They were clustered round Melanie, at the start of afternoon school, all agog to hear the bad news.

'What did she say?' urged Lol. 'Tell us what she said!'

'She *said*,' said Melanie, 'that if that was the best some people could do, then some people ought not to be in the show at all.'

'At all,' agreed Lol.

'At all!' breathed Ash.

'I can tell you,' said Melanie, 'in a professional theatre that sort of behaviour simply would not be tolerated. They would *all* have been given the Grand Order.'

'Grand Order!' breathed Ash.

'Grand Order?' said Lol.

'Of the boot,' said Melanie. 'In other words . . . *out*!'

Jo, frantically finishing off last night's French homework – which she hadn't been able to finish last night, being too busy learning lines, and what thanks did you

146

get? None whatsoever. Just a load of abuse – did her best to concentrate on *La Famille Dupont en Vacances* and cut out the sound of Melanie's voice.

Monsier et Madame Dupont ning ning ning yack yack yack yack *et ses deux enfants, Jean-Claude et Anne-Marie*, for a pizza –

Pizza? Jo's head jerked up in spite of itself.

' – tomorrow evening, after the dress rehearsal,' said Melanie. 'She can't take us on Saturday because of coming to supper with my uncle. I have already asked my uncle and he said that he would be enchanted.'

'Enchanted!'

'So Sarah said in that case she'd better take us tomorrow.'

'Tomorrow!'

'But only the Lost Boys,' urged Lol.

'Oh, yes! Only the Lost Boys.' Melanie gave one of her irritating tinkly laughs. 'She certainly wouldn't take the understudies . . . not after what happened just now.'

Lol and Ashley snickered, sycophantically.

'I'm really looking forward to it,' said Melanie. 'We're going to the Pizza Palace. It should be great.'

'If I were *you* . . . ' Barge slammed her desk lid with such vehemence that Jo's pen almost bounced out of her hand. 'If I were you,' said Barge, 'I wouldn't be so quick to count my chickens before they've hatched.'

Melanie's big grey eyes opened wide, like flowers unfurling in the sunshine. What *could* the creature be on about?

'Accidents can happen,' said Barge, darkly. 'You might yet fall down a flight of stairs and break a leg.'

Melanie's tinkle rang out, clear and happy.

'In the theatre,' she said, 'when you say "break a leg" it means good luck.'

'Ho, does it?' said Barge. She took out her *Dix Contes d'Aujourd'hui* and slapped it on to her desk. 'It may have escaped your notice,' said Barge, 'that just at present we do not happen to be in a theatre, we happen to be in a school. And when one says "break a leg" in *this* establishment,' said Barge, 'it means precisely that, i.e., snap your tibula or fibia, or whatever they are called, which to any *normal* person –' Barge's sarcasm was withering – 'would, I have to suppose, count as dire misfortune, unless, of course, one is the morbid sort of person who enjoys being an invalid or happens to be having a French lesson in approximately five minutes' time and has not done one's French homework, in which case I do not doubt that a broken leg would come in extremely handy, and look here, Jam, if you have finished may I just borrow your book for a sec?'

Jo obediently shunted it across.

'Jealousy,' observed Melanie, to her simpering shadows, 'is a terrible thing.'

'Terrible thing –'

'My uncle,' said Melanie, 'says he meets it all the time. He says that anyone who is successful has to learn to expect it. But I do think,' said Melanie, 'that it is sad. I hope, Jam, that you don't *mind* having to understudy me?'

Jo hoicked her bag off the floor and buried her head inside it.

'How about falling down a sewer?' she muttered.

'A nice deep one,' said Bozzy.

'All stinky,' said Jo.

'And slimy,' said Bozzy.

'And gungy –'

'And putrid –'

'And pongy –'

'And *foul*.'

'Sounds like a nice idea,' said Fij.

'Neil desperado,' said Bozzy.

The dress rehearsal was scheduled for the last two periods on Friday afternoon – one of which, for 8N, was English, the other Gym. Gym and English were Jo's two favourite subjects. Just her rotten mouldy luck! The Seventh Years, who were missing out on double Maths, were jubilant.

The dress rehearsal went as well as could be expected, given that the Twins had a joint fit of hysterics and Jo's head wouldn't fit into the teapot, at any rate not without a struggle, and Nadge came bounding on in the middle of someone else's scene and said a rude word. Jasmine didn't seem too worried.

'A bad dress rehearsal,' said Melanie, quoting no doubt from her uncle, 'means a good performance.'

'Well, exactly,' said Jasmine. 'It'll be all right on the night – *if* people pay attention to what they're supposed to be doing.'

The Twins chortled: Nadge pulled a face. Jo said,

149

'What happens if my head gets stuck in the teapot and won't come out?'

'Then you'll be teapotted!' said Sarah. They all thought it terribly funny. Melanie absolutely shrieked.

Stubbornly, Jo said: 'I'm practically suffocated in there.'

'Suffocating in the cause of Art,' said Sarah. 'That's a very noble thing, Jo.'

Melanie shrieked again.

'The teapot is too small,' said Jo.

'Or is the head too large?' Sarah pondered the question. 'Which do we need? A larger teapot or a smaller head?'

'If she were a real professional,' said Melanie, 'she'd put her head in clamps for the night to try and reduce it.'

'I haven't got any clamps,' said Jo, angrily.

Sarah fell about.

'It's all right, Jo.' Jasmine, taking pity, ruffled what was left of her hair. 'We'll get the props people working on it. You'll get your teapot. OK, everyone! That's the lot for now. See you tomorrow!'

Tomorrow was the big day, when all four Houses would perform in front of an audience. The running order was Nellie's and York in the afternoon, Sutton and Roper in the evening. For people who intended sitting through all four performances, tea was to be laid on in the Small Hall, with coffee and biscuits at the end of the evening while the judges deliberated and decided on the winner.

The judges this year were a local councillor, one of

the school governors, and the director of PADS, the Petersham Amateur Dramatic Society. There had been talk of asking Melanie's uncle to be chairman, but thankfully – because otherwise Melanie would have been quite impossible: she was bad enough as it was – it had been pointed out that it would be awkward for the chairman of the judges to have to judge his own niece.

'Not that he would ever indulge in favouritism,' said Melanie. 'He's far too professional for that.'

'Oh, but of *course*,' crooned Barge, at her most syrupy. 'I'm sure he wouldn't *dream* of it.'

'Well, he wouldn't,' protested Melanie; but she blushed as she said it, so that Jo bet there had been something going on. She bet it was Melanie trying to get in with Sarah. Not that she would actually *ask* her uncle to choose Nellie's as the winner – she wouldn't be that crude; she would just drop hints, like, 'Sarah's worked so-o-o-o hard, it means so-o-o-o much to her, she would be so-o-o-o thrilled', etc. And then Sarah would be in Melanie's debt and would say, 'Melanie, I simply cannot thank you enough! I'm eternally grateful to you! Where should I have been without you?' And Melanie would prink and preen even worse than ever.

Jo's heart raged and hammered. Why couldn't she have an uncle who was an actor instead of a boring bank person? Some people, it seemed to Jo, had all the luck.

Barge and Bozzy were waiting for her as she left school at the end of the dress rehearsal. They were sitting on the wall of the house next door (something whch was strictly against school rules), kicking their legs and munching packets of crisps (something else which was against school rules: eating in public was almost a worse crime than not doing your homework or being late for classes; as if eating, as Matty had once said, were something dirty like picking your nose). Jo was surprised to see them there. School had been let out half an hour ago, and it wasn't even as if they caught the same bus.

'We just thought we'd wait and find out how it had gone,' said Barge. 'Make sure you were all right.'

Jo was touched. 'As a matter of fact,' she said, 'I nearly wasn't . . . the teapot is too small. I nearly got my head stuck in it.'

Barge clucked, sympathetically. '*No* consideration. Can't even take the trouble to get you a teapot that fits properly.'

'And what, if anything,' said Bozzy, 'has That Woman done about her hair?'

Melanie's hair had been the big surprise of the dress rehearsal – a surprise, at any rate, to Jo. She had suddenly appeared with it all hacked off, so that it hung in shreds round her face and stuck out like bunches of twigs over her ears. Jo, without thinking, had shrieked, 'When did you get that done?' It hadn't been like it in class that morning; she must have sneaked out to a hairdresser in the lunch hour. Katy Wells and Jan Hammond had looked at her, pityingly. Sarah had laughed. Melanie, with a sly grin at Sarah, had said, 'That's my secret!' Jo had had the distinct feeling that it was a

152

secret everyone was in on except her. Jasmine had confirmed it.

'It's a wig, Jo . . . she wasn't brave enough to do what you did.'

'She's got a wig.' Jo said it bitterly. 'They actually hired one for her.'

'*Hired* one?'

'You mean they spent *money*?'

'On *Melanie*?'

They hadn't spent money on any of the other Lost Boys; they had all been chosen because they had short hair and looked boyish to begin with.

'It is almost unbelievable,' said Bozzy. 'When they could have had you for nothing!'

'Purely out of interest,' said Barge, 'a mere casual enquiry . . . who would play your part if you weren't able to? They have someone standing by, I suppose?'

'They'd just stick a Playing Card in.'

'In the teapot?' said Bozzy.

'Would it fit?' said Barge.

Jo looked at them, suspiciously. Were they trying to be funny?

'How should I know?' she said. 'Why, anyway?'

'Oh! No reason. One just wondered, that is all.'

They walked companionably, one on either side of her, up Shapcott Road.

'Now, you do know your lines, don't you?' said Barge, cosily.

'Lines?' said Jo. 'I haven't got any lines! All I get to say is twinkle twinkle twinkle, tw –'

'I don't mean the Dormouse's lines.' Barge spoke

153

gently, and with great patience. 'I mean Melanie's lines . . . Do you know Melanie's lines?'

'Yes, I do,' said Jo, savagely. 'I spent *hours* learning them and *no*body else bothered.' And Sarah hadn't even noticed.

'Good, good,' said Barge, nodding. 'I'm very glad to hear it.'

'Because after all,' said Bozzy, 'you never know when it might come in useful.'

'What, knowing someone else's lines?' Jo gave a short, sharp laugh, as close to Barge's sarcastic bark as it was possible to get.

'Be prepared,' said Barge. 'That is my motto.'

'Funny, I thought it was the Girl Guides',' said Jo.

'Theirs and mine both,' said Barge.

'Well, unless you happen to know of a handy open sewer –'

'All I am saying,' said Barge, soothingly, 'is that one should hold oneself in readiness.'

'Neil Desperado!' yelled Bozzy, walloping her rather hard on the back.

'Gerroff!' cried Jo. It didn't do to teach Bozzy these little pearls of wit and wisdom; she overdid them.

At nine o'clock that evening the telephone rang. Andy went off to answer it.

'For you,' he said, beckoning to Jo.

'Me?' said Jo. 'Who is it?'

'Aha!' said Andy. 'That would be telling.'

Sarah! she thought. Could it be Sarah? Ringing to say that Melanie had choked herself into an apoplexy stuffing too much pizza into her mouth and that Jo was going to have to play Slightly . . .

She snatched up the receiver.

'Hallo?'

'Hi, it's me,' said Robbie.

Jo felt like screaming.

'Why aren't you at the Club?'

'I don't *have* to come to the Club,' said Jo.

'N-no, of c-course not,' stammered Robbie. 'I d-didn't mean that. I m-m-m-m –'

'I couldn't be bothered,' said Jo, 'if you want to know. We had a dress rehearsal today and it went on for ever.'

'Oh. Y-yes. I s-see. Well, I'll – I'll s-see you tomorrow, then.'

'I suppose so,' said Jo.

'Well, I w-will,' said Robbie, 'because we're c-coming to the sh-sh-sh-sh-sh –'

'I know,' said Jo. 'You told me before.'

'D-did I? Oh, y-yes,' said Robbie. 'So I d-d-d –'

Jo held the receiver away from her ear. She wondered if Sarah's boyfriend, the great and glorious John Jestico, kept pestering her like this. Couldn't Robbie understand that she was *through* with boys? At any rate, for this term. Maybe next term she might feel differently; but just for the moment she could live without them. Why couldn't he read the signs? Did she have to be *rude* to him?

'Look, I have to go now,' she said. 'There's something I want to watch on television.'

'Well!' said Mrs Jameson, coming down the stairs on

155

her way from the bath. 'That's not a very polite way to talk to anyone.'

'It was only Robbie.'

'What do you mean, only Robbie? Robbie's a human being, isn't he, the same as anyone else? He has feelings, doesn't he? What's poor Robbie done to upset you?'

He hadn't done anything; he just *was*. 'He gets on my nerves,' muttered Jo.

'That's no excuse for being unkind to him. Good manners,' said Mrs Jameson, 'cost nothing.'

Actually, they did. When you were in the sort of mood that Jo was in, they cost a very great deal indeed; and right now Jo couldn't be bothered.

'Are you inviting him to Matty's party?'

'Matty's party is *Matty's* party. How can I invite someone to *Matty's* party?'

'I'm sure she'd let you if you asked her.'

'Well, I don't want to ask her! I don't want *him* hanging around.'

Mrs Jameson twitched an eyebrow. 'You want to watch it,' she said. 'You're in danger of becoming very unpleasant, my girl.'

There were times, thought Jo, when life was enough to make you so.

The following morning, when the post came, there was an envelope for Jo. Inside was a greetings telegram. It said, GOOD LUCK FOR TONIGHT LOVE ROBBIE.

'Well!' said Mrs Jameson. 'Isn't that nice of him? I

think that's really nice.' Her tone implied, *after the way you treated him* . . .

'I suppose so.' Jo said it grudgingly. She didn't want Robbie being nice to her: it put her under an obligation and meant she had to be nice back. She wasn't *feeling* nice.

'There aren't many boys who would have thought of that,' said Mrs Jameson.

'But it's stupid!' burst out Jo. 'I'm only playing a Dormouse!'

'Don't be so churlish and ungrateful! You should think yourself lucky someone cares enough to send you telegrams. *I* wouldn't send you telegrams, the way you've been behaving just lately.'

Jo sulked into her porridge, but because she was actually feeling a bit guilty she rang Robbie after breakfast, just to say thank you – only to discover that it hadn't been his idea to send the telegram but Barge's.

'*Barge*?' said Jo.

'That's what she said her name was.' Robbie sounded doubtful. 'She said she was a friend of yours.'

'But she doesn't know you!' said Jo.

'She said she got my number from Matty.'

'What is this?' said Jo, crossly. 'Some kind of a plot?'

'I don't think so,' said Robbie. 'I think she just wanted you to get a telegram.'

'So why couldn't she send me a telegram herself?'

'I guess –' Robbie said it apologetically – 'I guess she thought it would be b-better if I s-sent it.'

'Why?' said Jo.

'W-w-well –'

'She's *mad*,' said Jo, vehemently. 'All I'm playing is a Dormouse – all I do is *squeak*.'

'I'm s-sorry. I didn't m-mean to ups-set you.'

'It's not your fault,' said Jo. It was that maniac, Barge.

'I don't see why you're so angry,' said Tom.

Nor did Jo, when she stopped to think about it. She supposed it was something to do with having to force herself out of her crabby mood in order to be nice to Robbie and then discovering that she needn't have bothered because it hadn't been his idea anyway, and it was all completely idiotic because who ever heard of sending a telegram to someone who didn't even have any lines to say? It was *sick*.

She went next door to tackle Matty about it.

'Did Barge tell you *why* she wanted Robbie's number?'

'Yeah. She said she wanted to get him to send you a telegram.'

'I suppose you didn't think to ask her why she couldn't send me a telegram?'

'Not really,' said Matty. 'I just gave her his number. Why? Didn't you want a telegram?'

'It's like a bad joke!' cried Jo.

The curtain was due to go up at four o'clock on '*Peter Meets Alice*'. Jasmine had ordered all members of the cast to be in the building by no later than three-fifteen – 'We don't want any last-minute panics.'

By quarter to four, Jo was all ready and waiting, zipped into her Dormouse costume – a brown catsuit made of furry wool which came right up over her head like a Balaclava helmet, with a rubbery mask sewn on to it. The mask had a wriggly nose and whiskers, and big sticking-out teeth which made people laugh. Everyone said it was the best costume in the show. They didn't know how horribly hot and itchy it was.

Jo was sitting there, in the dressing room which she shared with the Playing Cards, twitching her whiskers in front of the mirror, when Jasmine poked her head round the door and in tones of consternation said, 'Has anyone seen Melanie?'

Jo shook her head. One of the Playing Cards said, 'I saw her in the cloakroom.'

'When was that?'

'Ages ago . . . when we first got here.'

'OK! I'll try there.'

Claire said, 'Maybe she's got locked in a lav.' She giggled, and started singing: 'Oh, dear, what can the matter be? Melanie Peach got locked in the lavatory. She was there all afternoon Saturday. And nobody, nobody cared!'

Jo twitched her whiskers. Several of the Playing Cards sniggered. Melanie had made herself unpopular just lately, with all her boasting about 'my uncle the actor'. Nobody probably *would* care if she were locked in a lavatory. Let her stay there.

'Best place for her!'

Except, of course, that the curtain was due to go up in a little over ten minutes. Jo's heart, unbidden, started thudding and hammering in her catsuit. Suppose – just suppose – that Melanie had fainted, or come over

159

peculiar, or suddenly got the great galloping collywobbles and run away to hide . . .

'Jo!' It was Jasmine back again. 'Goodness only knows what's happened to Melanie; we've got people out looking for her all over. You'd better get out of the costume and get into Slightly's. Here! If she turns up you can always do a quick change at the last minute. Claire, you're about Jo's size – can you take over as the Dormouse?'

Jo was out of one costume and into the other in a flash. She could hardly believe this was happening . . . she, Joanne Jameson, was playing a Lost Boy! She would be on stage with Sarah, not just stuck in a teapot but actually saying lines, actually doing real *acting*. Who knew? Perhaps Sarah might even ask if she could join Melanie (if Melanie was ever found) and her uncle and her uncle's girlfriend for supper after the show, seeing as she had missed out on last night's pizza. And if Melanie *wasn't* found – well, then, Jo and Sarah could go off to supper without her.

On legs gone all trembly with excitement, Jo wobbled out of the dressing room and made her way towards the Hall. Already she could hear the anticipatory buzz of conversation as the audience took their seats. How surprised her family would be when they saw Jo come bouncing on as Slightly! They would see Claire first of all, as the Dormouse, and would naturally assume that it was Jo. They would think they were seeing double when Slightly appeared!

Bozzy was dancing about at the stage door. Her face

160

was all scrumpled and pink; she seemed almost as excited as Jo.

'I told you,' she hissed. 'I *said* Neil Desperado!'

'Don't speak too soon,' said Jo, wondering at the same time how Bozzy had known. 'There's still another five minutes to go.'

'That's all right,' said Bozzy. 'She won't turn up now.'

'She could,' said Jo. She couldn't suppress an uncomfortable feeling that this wasn't *like* Melanie. Melanie prided herself on being a professional – she was always lecturing the rest of them for behaving like amateurs. Professionals didn't disappear half an hour before the curtain was due to go up. And while the great galloping collywobbles theory was appealing, it didn't really ring true, even to Jo's prejudiced ears.

'Look, just don't worry about her,' said Bozzy. 'This is your Big Chance!'

'Yes, I know,' said Jo. 'But I wonder what's happened to her?'

'I'll tell you what's happened to her,' said Bozzy. She glanced over her shoulder to make sure no one was around, then put her mouth close to Jo's ear: 'She's fallen down a sewer . . . '

13

'A *sewer*?' said Jo.

'A sewer,' giggled Bozzy.

'But how? I mean, when? I mean – how do you *know*?' said Jo.

Bozzy just giggled and didn't reply. Jo looked at her, suspiciously.

'You've done something!'

'Might have,' giggled Bozzy. 'Might not.'

'You have. You've been up to something!'

'All right,' giggled Bozzy, 'so we've been up to something.'

'What? What have you been up to? Tell me!' demanded Jo. 'Tell me what you've done!'

Bozzy was giggling so much she was hiccuping. Jo could have shaken her.

'*Tell me!*'

'We wrote her a' (giggle) 'note and left it on her peg in the' (hic!) 'cloakroom saying that Sarah' (hic, giggle) 'wanted to see her immediately in the Gym –' (hic!)

'And then what happened?' said Jo; though she had a horrid feeling that she could guess.

'Then –' Bozzy wiped her nose across the sleeve of her sweater – 'then she w-went up to the Gym and –'

'*And*?' said Jo.

'And we locked her in!' howled Bozzy, the tears streaming down her cheeks.

'You maniacs!' screamed Jo.

Bozzy went staggering off along the corridor, reeling drunkenly from side to side as fresh waves of hiccups and giggles assailed her. Jo, her brain whirring feverishly, was left on her own at the stage door. Two of the Playing Cards passed her, followed by Claire, in the Dormouse suit.

'They still haven't found her,' said Claire.

No, and they never would, if she was locked in the Gym. The Gym was not only soundproofed, because of being above classrooms, it was way over on the far side of the building, where no one would ever think of looking. Of course she wouldn't come to any harm; there was plenty of air, and it wasn't very likely that she would starve, even if she were left there all weekend. Not that she would be, because presumably Barge and Bozzy would go and let her out once the show was over, and even if they didn't, Jo certainly would. Knowing Melanie, she probably wouldn't be frightened; she would be too cross to be frightened. Jo pictured her rattling at the door and shouting, and maybe even climbing up the wall bars to bang on the windows and wave. It wouldn't do her any good. The windows looked out on to the playing field, and who would be on the playing field on the day of the inter-house drama? Melanie was going to be angry as a hornet, especially as her uncle was in the audience. She had been going on about her uncle for weeks.

I 'specially want my uncle to see what I can do. . . .

My uncle said he's really interested to see me on stage. . . . My uncle hasn't seen me do anything since Juniors.

And now her uncle wouldn't be seeing her, he would be seeing Jo instead. Jo wondered why she wasn't feeling more jubilant about it. After all, Melanie deserved to be lured into the Gym and locked up. She had been totally unbearable ever since being cast as Slightly. She had been arrogant, she had been boastful, and she had been patronizing. Worst of all, she had curried favour with Sarah. On the other hand . . .

Jo frowned, and swallowed. She couldn't help thinking how she would feel, if someone came along and locked her up on what was supposed to be her big day. Also, though it wasn't something she liked to admit, Melanie was actually very good as Slightly. She might not look much like a boy in real life, but on stage she became someone quite different. The way she swaggered and strutted, you would never know she was the same flabby creature who did belly flops over the box and fell off the parallel bars and whinged about climbing the ropes because she said it hurt her hands.

'It doesn't look as if she's going to turn up now,' said Claire. She scratched at her neck. 'This thing feels as if it's made out of *thistles*. I don't know how you stand it.'

Jo didn't know how she stood it, either. A mouldy Dormouse, stuck inside a prickly thistle suit with her head in a teapot . . .

'Hey! Where are you off to?' cried Claire.

164

'Won't be a minute!' Jo flapped a hand. 'Just had an idea!'

Down the corridor she ran, ignoring the angry shouts of Michelle Wandres and the surprised glances of parents on their way into the Hall; up the side stairs by the games cupboard, along the passage past the Music Rooms, round the corner and up a second flight of stairs to the Gym. She paused, panting, outside the door. Not a sound could be heard. Was Melanie really in there? Or had Bozzy been having her on?

The Gym door had large, old-fashioned bolts top and bottom: sure enough, the bottom bolt had been pushed into place. (They obviously hadn't been able to reach the top one.) With some difficulty, because the bolt was stiff, she managed to heave it back. Even before she had a chance to turn the handle, the door had been wrenched open from the other side and Melanie came flouncing out.

'Quick!' gasped Jo. She set off again, at a gallop.

'Just a minute!' Melanie caught at Jo's arm. 'How did you know I was in there?'

'Oh – ah –' Jo hadn't thought of that. 'I – um – heard someone say that they'd seen you come up here.'

Melanie narrowed her eyes. 'Who?'

'Oh! Someone. I can't remember, everything was in such a panic. Sarah said I'd have to go on in your place and –'

'And then, I suppose –' Melanie's lip curled – 'you got stage fright and thought you'd better come and let me out.'

'Stage fright?' Jo's cheeks reddened; partly at the

unfairness of it – stage fright had had absolutely nothing to do with it – partly at the implication that Jo had known all along about Melanie being locked in the Gym. It was just near enough to the truth to make her feel uncomfortable.

'I don't know what Sarah's going to say,' said Melanie.

That was something else Jo hadn't thought of. She began to wonder whether it might not have been better to have left Melanie where she was; it would certainly have been less complicated.

'She's bound to want to know who this mysterious person was that saw me go up there . . . I suppose it couldn't have been the same mysterious person who slammed the door and ran away?'

'Goodness!' Jo attempted a laugh. 'I shouldn't think so. I should think what happened, I should think a member of staff saw the door wasn't properly shut and didn't realize anyone was in there and thought they'd better bolt it. In case of burglars,' said Jo. 'I expect they *do* bolt it. Sometimes. 'Specially at weekends.'

'Tell that to Sarah!' said Melanie.

Backstage was in chaos – two minutes to curtain up and now the Dormouse had disappeared as well as Slightly.

'She *said*,' said Claire, 'that she'd just had a –'

'Jo!' screamed Jasmine. 'You've found her!'

Sarah, dressed in her Peter costume, sprang round.

'Where have you been? We've been looking everywhere for you!'

166

Melanie opened her mouth. 'I have been locked,' she said, 'in the –'

'Quick!' cried Sarah. 'Get into your costume! Jo, give Melanie her costume back! I'll see if I can get them to hold the curtain for a few seconds.'

'You are all right, are you?' said Jasmine. 'Or would you rather Jo went on?'

Jo had never seen Melanie move so fast. There in front of everybody she tore off her clothes, snatched her costume from Jo, her wig from Jasmine, who had run to fetch it, and within seconds was transformed from pretty pouting Melanie (in a pretty pouting rage) to the amiable simpleton, Slightly.

Jo, stripped practically naked, was left shivering and unregarded in a corner, waiting for Claire to surrender the thistle suit.

Everyone said afterwards that 'Peter Meets Alice' was brilliant; that Sarah was brilliant, that Melanie was brilliant, that Alice was lovely, that the Mad Hatter and the March Hare were hilarious, that the Lost Boys were incredibly boylike and the Playing Cards were 'a touch of class'. Oh, yes, and the Dormouse was cute/sweet/cuddly/fun. But it was Sarah and Melanie who were the undoubted stars of the show. Sarah took a special curtain call with Alice, while Melanie only took one with the other Lost Boys, but that didn't stop people talking of her as if she were one of the leads.

If Jo hadn't gone and got a conscience and felt sorry for her, they might have been talking of Jo as if she were one of the leads. Sarah might have been saying, even now, 'Jo, you were fantastic! I don't know what we should have done without you.' Melanie, of course, would still have been locked in the Gym, but who would have cared about that? Certainly not Jo. She must have been mad, going and letting her out. Melanie wasn't in the least bit grateful, and Sarah, the one person who mattered, would never know the sacrifice that she had made.

Jo changed out of her costume and back into her own clothes as fast as ever she could, then scudded off up the corridor and into the Hall in time to see the curtain go up on York's monumentally boring offering, 'A Greek Tragedy in One Act'. York were always boring and Jo had absolutely no interest whatsoever in Greek tragedy, but anything was preferable to being got at by Melanie demanding all over again to know who the mysterious person was who had seen her going up to the Gym.

As soon as the curtain came down, Jo made a dive for the doors, only to be yanked back, unceremoniously, not to say brutally, by Michelle Wandres, who accused her of having no manners and being a disgusting little beast, 'trying to get to the tea things ahead of everyone else'. Tea couldn't have been further from Jo's mind: she had been going to go and hide in the lavatory.

'You can stay here,' said Michelle, 'and smile at people and try for once to be civil.'

Jo stood there, grimacing, poised precariously on one leg, with the other wrapped round it.

'I said *smile*,' snarled Michelle, 'not look as if you're about to throw up!'

On sudden inspiration, Jo said: 'Actually, I think I am . . . I think I need to go *immediately*.'

She managed to get halfway to the cloakroom before being ambushed by Barge and Bozzy.

'Are you out of your mind?' shrieked Barge.

'Ingratitude!' shrilled Bozzy.

'Shut up!' said Barge. 'It was your fault for going and opening your big mouth in the first place!'

'Well, how was I to know? *I* didn't know she'd be stupid enough to let her out!'

'If you hadn't told her where she was, there wouldn't have been any question of her letting her out.'

'I thought we could trust her!' whined Bozzy.

'Be more to the point if I could trust *you*!' snapped Barge.

It was this juncture that Jo saw Melanie looming on the horizon, coming at her from the direction of the cloakroom. She turned and fled, taking refuge in the crowds heading towards the Small Hall, where tea was laid out. In the Hall she was instantly cornered by Robbie, wanting to tell her how good she had been.

'I thought you were far and away the best thing in it . . . honestly.'

Jo had a moment of blind fury. She *might* have been one of the best things in it if it hadn't been for her idiotic conscience. There were times when it seemed to Jo that it wasn't worth having a conscience. You didn't get any thanks, you just made a whole load of trouble for yourself.

'You were,' said Robbie. 'You were really good.'

'What about Sarah?' said Jo.

'Which one was Sarah?'

'The one who helped write it – the one who played Peter.'

'Oh, well, yes. Of course. *She* was good.'

'What about Melanie?'

'Is she the one whose uncle's Tracey Peach?' Even Robbie knew about Melanie's uncle. 'Well, she would be good, wouldn't she? I mean . . . ' Robbie faltered. 'I mean, she wasn't any better than *you*.'

'Yes, she was,' said Jo. It would be hard not to be better than someone who had her head stuck in a teapot all the time. Across the room, a queue was forming. She craned, trying to see what it was for. All she could make out was the top of a man's head as he sat at a table.

'That's Tracey Peach,' said Robbie.

Oh, so *that* was him, thought Jo. There didn't seem to be any sign of the famous girlfriend. She'd probably walked out on him.

'He's signing autographs,' said Robbie.

Jo looked, and saw that Tom was there in the queue, pen and paper at the ready. Tom was such a creep. When she'd told him, once, about Melanie's uncle, he'd pretended never to have heard of him, and when she'd said he was in 'Lovat Lane' he'd denied ever watching the programme, which she'd known at the time was a lie because she'd actually caught him at it. Tom had said grandly that that was 'when I was *young*. I wouldn't watch it now. It's a load of crap.' But he couldn't resist going creeping and crawling for an autograph.

170

'Don't you want one?' said Robbie.

'You must be joking,' said Jo. She wouldn't lower herself. 'You get one,' she said, 'if you want.'

'I don't want one for me,' said Robbie. 'It's for my cousin.'

That was what they all said, Melanie had told them: *it's for my sister, my cousin, my auntie, my mum . . .* silly load of sheep.

'It is,' said Robbie. 'She's a fan of "Lovat Lane". She watches it all the time.'

'Well, go on, then!' If there was one thing Jo couldn't stand, it was a ditherer. 'Go and get it! What's stopping you?'

'I'll be right back,' said Robbie.

He wouldn't be right back, the queue was at least thirty deep – and oh, heavens! There was Melanie, simpering up to the head of it to attach herself to her uncle and grab a bit of the limelight. At least Sarah hadn't gone all creepy-crawly. Jo could see Sarah with John Jestico and a man and woman who must be her mum and dad – the famous Dr Bigg, who was so brilliant. He didn't look brilliant. He looked rather small and bald and insignificant. And Sarah's mum looked just like anyone else's mum. Jo stared round for her own family and spotted them in a corner, talking – horror of horrors! – to Mrs Stanley. Mrs Stanley would be telling them how dire Jo's Maths was. She wasn't going over *there*.

Out of the corner of her eye she saw Barge and Bozzy come bundling back into the Hall and make a beeline for her. Jo turned, in a panic, burrowed blindly

171

through the crowd and fetched up with a bump against Fij.

'Oh, there you are!' said Fij. 'I've been looking for you.'

'Quick! Hide me!' panted Jo. 'They're after me!'

'Who's after you?'

'Barge and Bozzy!' Jo hustled Fij out through one of the side doors. 'They're mad at me for letting Melanie out.'

Fij looked blank. 'Out where?'

'Out of the Gym.'

'Out of the *Gym*?'

'They locked her in –'

'Locked her *in*?'

'Yes, and then I went and let her out and now they're mad at me.'

'What did they lock her in for?'

'So that I could play Slightly, and now they're saying I'm ungrateful, and Melanie didn't even thank me for it – she said I must have got stage fright, which was absolutely untrue, I just felt sorry for her, and now I almost wish I hadn't bothered, I wish I'd just left her there to moulder and rot, and oh, help! Here they come again!'

Jo turned and dived back into the Hall, almost knocking over a small child. As she passed the tea table, she grabbed at a sandwich and a couple of buns, and to the amazement of a watching parent began stuffing them into her mouth. Choking and spluttering and spraying crumbs, Jo headed back for the main exit.

She spent the rest of the interval locked in a lavatory in the downstairs cloakroom.

At half-past six the curtain went up on Roper's offering. Jo slunk into the Hall at the last minute and perched herself at the very end of the back row. Roper's were never very imaginative. They had dramatized a Russian short story by someone Jo hadn't heard of and spent the whole forty minutes being intense and gloomy, going round in false beards pretending to be Russians, saying things like, 'What a sad business this is, Ivan Ivanovitch.'

Sutton's came as a welcome relief. Their piece was a spoof romance called 'The Moon in June' by Lou C. Love. It was quite amusing and clever, but Lou C. Love was obviously a committee rather than a person and the piece was more of a series of sketches than a proper play. There wasn't any doubt in Jo's mind who the overall winner was going to be.

Tom, of course, had to argue about it. When Jo risked going into the Small Hall afterwards for her biscuits and coffee (if she stuck with her family not even Barge and Bozzy, surely, would dare come pushing themselves in) she found him loudly declaring that in his opinion Roper's ought to win because 'they were so boring they were funny'. An old man sitting behind him, Tom said, had gone to sleep and snored, and when his wife had woken him up he'd given a loud snort and said, 'I thought it would never end!'

'I don't see anything particularly funny about that,' said Jo.

'What was funny,' gasped Tom, going into parox-

173

ysms at the memory of it, 'was that it had only just begun!'

Jo turned contemptuously away.

'I think yours was the best,' said Robbie, who had come over to join them. 'So do my mum and dad, and so does my sister. And we thought you were the best thing in it,' he added, loyally.

Jo did wish he wouldn't. It was *stupid*.

'He's only trying to be nice to you,' said Mrs Jameson, as Robbie went back to his own family.

'Yes,' said Jo. 'I know.'

'I do think you might try to be just a little nicer back.'

Jo sighed. 'Perhaps I will . . . next term.'

At half-past eight they all trouped back into the Main Hall to hear the judges' verdict. Although he wasn't anything to do with the actual judging, Melanie's uncle had been asked to go up on stage and make the announcement.

He bounded three at a time up the steps – to show that he was still young and athletic, Jo supposed – and gracefully glided to the centre of the stage. He was very tall and dark and handsome (though not as handsome as John Jestico) and he spoke in a deep actorish voice that boomed about the Hall.

He had tremendously enjoyed all four of the shows, he said; but – with an eager, boyish grin – he wasn't there to deliver *his* verdict but the verdict of the judges. And the verdict of the judges – making a great show of consulting a small slip of paper – the verdict of the judges, by a clear majority, was that 'Peter Meets Alice'

174

was the winner, followed by 'The Moon in June' as runner-up.

'I have been asked that the co-authors of the winning piece – Sarah Bigg, who receives a commendation for her portrayal of Peter, and Jasmine Patel, who directed – should come up on the platform, please.'

To a great outburst of clapping, Sarah and Jasmine went up on stage. One of the judges then stepped forward, holding up a hand for silence.

'Before you give these two young ladies the applause they so richly deserve, may I just beg leave to make one final announcement? We all felt – but wished to spare Mr Peach any possible embarrassment, which is why you're having to put up with me for a moment instead of him – that we should like to make special mention of the performance of Melanie Peach, who played Slightly. Melanie, as I expect some of you may already know, is in fact related to Mr Peach – your niece, if I am not mistaken?' Melanie's uncle graciously inclined his head. 'I wish to stress that that, however, had absolutely no bearing on our decision, which was made absolutely unanimously; though I daresay –' big broad gushy beam – 'that thespian talent does run in the family!' Sycophantic laughter from all and sundry (except Jo). 'So, Melanie . . . step up here and be congratulated!'

Melanie needed no second invitation. She was out of her seat and up on the platform on jet-propelled legs almost before Jo had a chance to blink. They stood there, in a row – Jasmine, Sarah and Melanie – while

175

the audience clapped themselves silly. Even the judges joined in. Melanie's uncle clapped louder than anyone.

'Honestly,' whispered Robbie, in Jo's ear, 'you were just as good as she was . . .'

14

'Don't forget my party,' said Matty to Jo, as they walked up to the bus together after the weekend, on the last day of term.

Matty was having her party on the day after Boxing Day. She had chosen it specially 'to cheer people up between Christmas and New Year'.

'Who've you asked?' said Jo.

'Jool, Nadge, you –' Matty ticked them off as she spoke. 'Meta, Dillon, Miles –' Miles was Matty's brother, Meta and Dillon were her cousins. Matty had been sweet on Dillon at one time, but not any longer. '*Tom*. I have to have Tom,' said Matty, in tones that implied she would rather not (Jo knew how she felt), 'because of someone to keep Miles company. And anyway my mum says I've got to. She says it would be rude not to.'

'Why would it be rude not to?' said Jo, thinking that in fact it would be rather nice.

'Don't ask me,' said Matty. 'Are you going to bring Robbie?'

'Robbie?' Jo crinkled her nose. 'I thought we weren't into boys any more?'

'Well, *I'm* not,' said Matty, 'but Jool's got her cousin staying, which means *he's* got to come, and *Tom's* got

177

to come, and then there's Dillon, and then there's Miles . . . I just thought,' said Matty, 'we might as well have even numbers. That way there's more chance they'll leave us alone.'

'Mm.' Jo rubbed a finger across her forehead. 'I suppose so.'

'So what do you reckon?' said Matty.

'I'll think about it,' said Jo.

She had made a mental promise to be nicer to Robbie *next term*; but the Christmas holidays weren't next term and inviting him to a party would simply be encouraging him. Robbie didn't need encouraging; he was soppy enough as it was.

'I'll let you know,' said Jo.

When they arrived at school they found Melanie in the classroom, basking in Saturday's glory and recounting in colourful detail how 'my uncle and Sarah and me' had all gone out to supper to celebrate after the show.

Jo clattered busily at her desk, stacking her books ready to be handed in, rounding up paperclips and all the stray bits and pieces that tended to accumulate during the course of a term. What was a disgusting great wad of chewing gum doing in there? Jo never ate chewing gum. Ugh! It was revolting. Full of someone else's horrible teeth marks and someone else's noxious spit. She scraped it off and lobbed it towards the bin at the front of the room.

She hadn't intended it to whack Melanie in the face. A great cheeer went up from the denizens of the back row – Barge, Bozzy and the Bookends. Even Fij had to suppress a titter.

'Joanne Jameson!' screeched Melanie. 'Do you mind keeping your loathsome gob balls to yourself?'

'It wasn't mine,' said Jo.

'No, like it wasn't you on Saturday, I suppose?'

'What wasn't her on Saturday?' Ashley and the Lollipop were instantly agog.

'She knows,' said Melanie. 'Or if she doesn't –' she looked hard at Barge and Bozzy – 'somebody does.'

Barge regarded her haughtily. Bozzy popped her eyes.

'Fortunately,' said Melanie, 'coming as I do from a theatrical background, I realize that one has to be prepared for envy and for jealousy. As my uncle says, it's the price of fame . . . one's rivals will stop at nothing.'

Bozzy hummed a little song to herself.

'What *is* the creature wittering about?' said Barge.

'My uncle,' said Melanie, 'once knew an actor whose understudy put rat poison in his water jug.'

Gratifying gasps from Ashley and the Lollipop. One of the Bookends made a rude noise.

'What happened?' said Matty.

'Well, it's a very moral story,' said Melanie. 'He noticed it with the first sip, which normally he wouldn't have done because normally he would have mixed it with whisky. But it just so happened,' said Melanie, relishing both the tale and the fact that she had got herself an audience, 'that that very night he had decided to give up the demon drink and thus he was

179

saved. Which was just as well because if the understudy had had to go on he'd have been bound to get cold feet. Understudies,' said Melanie, not even bothering to look in Jo's direction, 'always do.'

The remark rankled. It had rankled on Saturday, and it continued to niggle for the rest of the morning. It niggled as they handed in books, it niggled as they tidied the classroom. It was still niggling as they filed out for the final Assembly.

'I didn't get cold feet!' hissed Jo.

Melanie grinned. 'I know you didn't, but it makes a good story . . . my uncle thought it was hilarious!'

Indignation swelled within Jo's breast. If Melanie had told her uncle, did that mean she had also told Sarah? Did it mean they had sat there, all three of them, stuffing their supper and enjoying themselves at Jo's expense?

Sarah was sitting on the platform behind Miss Durndell with the other House captains. Even at this moment she was probably inwardly sniggering. The *humiliation* of it, thought Jo. She had become nothing but a laughing stock.

She sat glumly through Miss Durndell's usual end-of-term round-up: Miss Kapinski getting married, Mrs Winter leaving, Anna Wong winning music prize, someone else winning poetry prize, Nellie's winning drama competition, Sarah Bigg and Jasmine Patel highly recommended, Melanie Peach special mention, school colours awarded, first team Susie Allport, under-14s Nadia Foster and Lee Powell, under-13s Joanne Jameson –

180

Joanne Jameson?????? Jo sat there, stunned. A sharp dig in the ribs from Fij brought her to her senses.

'Well, go on! Get up there!'

Jo tottered out of her seat. On legs of cardboard, she stumbled up the gangway. On the platform stood Miss Durndell, patiently waiting, colours in hand. Jo's colours!

Jo felt a sudden burst of confidence. Joyously, three at a time like Melanie's uncle, she bounded up the steps. Unfortunately, unlike Melanie's uncle, she didn't bother to look where she was going: the school applauded loudly as Jo pitched forward on to Sarah's lap . . .

'Get up, Jo, for goodness' sake!' muttered Sarah. 'Don't make more of an idiot of yourself than you have to.'

Sarah thought she had done it on purpose! Cheeks awash in a sea of crimson, Jo staggered to her feet and lurched across to Miss Durndell.

'Well!' said Miss Durndell, who was not above making little jokes every now and again. 'It's to be hoped you're more adept on the netball court!'

On the last day of term, members of the lower forms were allowed, if they wished, to present themselves at the door of the Prefects' Room and ask for autographs. It was the one occasion when making a nuisance of yourself was tolerated and not even Michelle Wandres had the power to complain or dish out order marks.

'Are you going to go and knock?' said Fij, as she and Jo left the Hall together at the end of Assembly.

Jo shook her head. After what had just happened? She wouldn't dare!

'Do you want me to?' said Fij. 'I don't mind doing it . . . give me your autograph book and I'll go and ask her for you.'

Jo sat in the classroom, on top of her empty desk, trying not to chew her nails as she waited for Fij to come back. To her right the Bookends were squabbling noisily over possession of a tatty packet of paper handkerchiefs; to the right Barge and Bozzy were having a high-flown intellectual discussion as to whether swallowing cherry stones, which Bozzy claimed to have done in vast quantities, could give you appendicitis. Jo, when appealed to, said vaguely that she imagined only time would tell, a response which successfully united them in scorn and contempt.

'Really,' said Barge, 'can't you be more precise?'

'How *much* time?' said Bozzy. 'A month? A year? A century?'

'Just as long as it takes, I suppose,' said Jo.

Barge and Bozzy exchanged glances.

'One thing I will say for you,' said Barge, magnanimously, to Bozzy, 'at least you are not afraid to speak your mind.'

'At least,' agreed Bozzy, proudly, 'I have opinions.'

'What I cannot *stand*,' said Barge, 'is people who are too woffly to come down on one side or the other.'

'Don't you have anything useful to say on the subject at *all*?' said Bozzy.

'Not really. Not being a doctor.' Jo slid off her desk and headed for the door. At any other time she might

182

have humoured them, but she had just seen Fij coming back along the passage. She darted out to meet her. 'Well?' said Jo.

Fij shook her head apologetically. 'She wouldn't give it me . . . she said if you want her autograph you'll have to go and ask for it.'

'I can't!' wailed Jo.

'You'll have to,' said Fij. 'She's kept your autograph book . . .'

It was Sarah herself who answered Jo's rather timorous knock.

'Ah, Jo,' she said. 'This is what you've come for, I presume?'

She held out Jo's autograph book – open, so that Jo could see what she had written. *To Jo, too honest to be Slightly. With thanks, from Sarah.*

Jo looked up, wondering, and a bit pink.

'Melanie told me,' said Sarah, 'how you went to her rescue. I shan't enquire too closely as to how you knew where to find her, but I am very glad that you did.'

'It wasn't because I had stage fright!' said Jo.

'I never imagined for one moment that it was. I assumed,' said Sarah, 'that it was because you had a sense of fair play – which is no more than I would expect from someone who has just got her school colours.'

Jo, by now, was as pink as a peony.

'And well deserved, too,' said Sarah.

'Thank you very much for nominating me,' said Jo.

'Oh, don't thank me! It wasn't anything to do with me. It's Jayne – Miss Duncan – you should be thanking.

183

I'm afraid I've been a bit slack this term, where games are concerned. "Peter and Alice" rather got the better of me. I hope –' Sarah paused. 'I hope that next term,' she said, 'we shall both manage to curb some of our wilder impulses.'

'I'm really sorry,' blurted Jo, 'if I've got on your nerves.'

'Well, you have,' said Sarah, 'but I shouldn't let it worry you too much, if I were you. We've all been there.'

Jo looked at her doubtfully.

'Try taking a peek in the games cupboard sometime,' advised Sarah, 'if you want to see a sample of my juvenile handiwork . . . left-hand corner of the top shelf underneath the cricket pads. Of course, I'm swearing you to secrecy!'

Left-hand corner of the top shelf, underneath the cricket pads . . .

JAYNE DUNCAN

The name leapt out at her. It was scored deep into the woodwork, heavily inked in with black felt-tip pen. Miss Duncan! Sarah had had a thing about Miss Duncan! She must have stood there in the games cupboard for hours, patiently carving. Or maybe she had done it bit by bit, over the weeks. Jo had never gone that far. But then, maybe Sarah had never gone as far as trying to rescue Miss Duncan from a bolting horse or fallen at her feet in a crumpled heap. She wished she could ask her, but probably it might embarrass her, because these things were rather embarrassing when you looked back on them; and anyway it was enough to know that Sarah had been there. Jo pushed the cricket pads back into place. She wasn't the only one who had made an idiot of herself!

That afternoon when she arrived back from school, Jo rang Robbie. He sounded surprised and pleased and nervous all at once when he heard who it was.

'I was just wondering,' said Jo, 'if you'd like to come to Matty's party with me, day after Boxing Day.'

There was a small silence.

'Wouldn't I be in the way?' said Robbie.

'Of course you wouldn't be in the way!' said Jo. 'Tom's going to be there, and Miles, and Dillon, and a cousin of Jool's. There'll be loads of other boys besides you.'

'Well, if you're really sure,' said Robbie.

'Course I'm sure!' said Jo. 'Wouldn't ask you if I wasn't, would I?'

'So you've decided to be nicer to him?' said Mrs Jameson as Jo came off the phone. 'I'm glad about that. I felt really sorry for that young man.'

'Well –' Jo humped a shoulder – 'one has to be tolerant. After all,' she said, 'we've all been there.'

Join the RED FOX Reader's Club

The Red Fox Readers' Club is for readers of all ages. All you have to do is ask your local bookseller or librarian for a Red Fox Reader's Club card. As an official Red Fox Reader you will qualify for your own Red Fox Reader's Clubpack – full of exciting surprises! If you have any difficulty obtaining a Red Fox Readers' Club card please write to: Random House Children's Books Marketing Department, 20 Vauxhall Bridge Road, London SW1V 2SA.